NOS

DATE DUE

MAY 04

7-21-04			
7-15-04			
7-21-04			
L 8 06			
4-3-07			
6/3/18			
GAYLORD			PRINTED IN U.S.A.

D1053688

Face
in the
Pond

Face
in the
Pond

Clarissa Ross

THORNDIKE
CHIVERS

This Large Print edition is published by Thorndike Press®,
Waterville, Maine USA and by BBC Audiobooks, Ltd,
Bath, England.

Published in 2004 in the U.S. by arrangement with
Maureen Moran Agency.

Published in 2004 in the U.K. by arrangement
with the author.

U.S. Hardcover 0-7862-6370-9 (Romance)
U.K. Hardcover 0-7540-9869-9 (Chivers Large Print)

The text of this Large Print edition is unabridged.
Other aspects of the book may vary from the original edition.

Set in 16 pt. Plantin by Elena Picard.

Printed in the United States on permanent paper.

British Library Cataloguing-in-Publication Data available

ISBN 0-7862-6370-9 (lg. print : hc : alk. paper)

Face in the Pond

1

It was the day of summing up!

The shafts of pale afternoon sunlight filtered through the tall leaded glass windows ranged along the left wall of the Edinburgh High Court of Justiciary on this May day in 1870. The pattern of light was coldly impartial as it fell on areas of the crowded spectator benches; the lordly bewigged prosecution, thumbs tucked in his black robes; the elderly bent defense, with his crafty eye; and the demure raven-haired accused who had sat through the many days of her trial for murder with quiet resignation. Her exquisite oval face under the brown cupped bonnet had shown little expression all through her ordeal.

Now the packed courtroom was rapt with attention as the arrogant young prosecutor made his closing address to the jury. The Lord Chief Justice, whose rather sympathetic wrinkled face was not made severe by his impressive wig, leaned on his right hand with a somewhat bored expression as if to hint to the jury that he was taking the prosecutor's vividly colored condemnation with the proverbial grain of salt, and they might do the same if they liked.

The accused, Sarah Bennett, let her eyes rove about the crowded spectator benches for a moment as the prosecutor thundered on and she felt a chilling fear because of what she saw. This motley crew, which included the dregs of the back-street slums and some of the city's most elegant and fashionable Princes Street ladies and gentlemen, were hanging on the prosecutor's every word with greedy excitement. The gargoyle faces of the poor and debased in common with the aloof aristocratic features of the gentility showed cruelty, curiosity, and apathy. There was no sympathy there.

But, yes, there was! Her opinion changed swiftly as her lovely green eyes came to rest on that familiar face. The face that had offered her the one true and consistent show of sympathy through all the endless days of her torment. He was a man in his early thirties, with a handsome, sensitive face, striking golden hair, keen blue eyes, and a strange pallor.

He had somehow managed to occupy almost the same seat in the courtroom day after day, although space was at a premium. She had been told that hundreds besieged the doors for entrance every morning and many were turned away. Yet he had always been there to reassure her with his soberly encouraging glance.

Or had she merely imagined this? Was the handsome young man merely a thrill-seeker like the others bent on satisfying his unwholesome appetites with this sordid exposure of her personal life and the twisted picture of what had happened as presented by the prosecutor? She didn't think so. Stranger that he was, she was certain he must be her only friend among all those so avidly listening and greedily enjoying the tale of love and violence at second hand.

Somewhat comforted by the thought that she was not completely alone, that this good soul was there once again to sustain her, she allowed herself the dubious luxury of listening to the prosecutor. Mostly she closed her ears to his words, but now he was at the end of his plea to the jury.

Corpulent face flushed, regal in his robes and stance, he directed a graceful hand in her direction, and in a sneering tone said, "Let me suggest you take a good look at this young woman, gentlemen of the jury!

Beneath the fragile tea-china beauty there is concealed the strength and venom of a jealous woman capable of murder. Do not be deceived by her delicate looks, but consider her icy demeanor during the time of this trial. There lies the key to her true nature — cold, hard, unyielding!"

He hunched his shoulders slightly and paused for a moment, inserting his thumbs in his gown again. "This is Sarah Bennett, the girl whom Amelia and John Gordon befriended! The girl they took into their fine home in Glasgow as nurse for their only child, a four-year-old daughter. This is the girl who mistakenly considering her employer's kindness to be the overtures of a man in love, became obsessed with a flaming passion to take the place of his wife.

"The good wife and mother, Amelia Gordon, was soon aware of the girl's jealousy of her and her unhealthy passion for her husband. Wanting to give Sarah Bennett every possible chance, she brought the matter into the open and advised the accused she must change her ways if she wished to continue living in their home and acting as nurse to the innocent child."

The prosecutor paused to glare at Sarah, and then resumed his address to the jury, "Was the accused grateful? Did she burst into the same tears that were streaming down the face of her considerate mistress and beg her forgiveness? She did not! No, gentlemen, she exhibited the same cold demeanor we have seen in this courtroom. She denied the charges and went about seeking the favors of John Gordon with a new avidity! Consider then, the chaos of bleak misery into which this hitherto happy household was thrown by this pretty but scheming miss!"

The prosecutor cleared his throat and gave both the spectators and jury a chance to relax. This was the signal for a cacophony of coughs and sneezes, and creaking of seats from all directions. The Lord Chief Justice closed his eyes briefly looking eminently bored, the attorney for the defense stared down at the floor in mild deference, and Sarah swept her glance to the sympathetic face of the blond man and was relieved to note that he still exhibited his kindly feelings toward her.

Having given his audience their moment of physical indulgence, the stern prosecutor spoke in a tense fashion to grasp their attention once again: "Now we enter upon the dark period of our sad tale. We have shown that Sarah Bennett made overtures to the shocked John Gordon, and that he repudiated her. So the wanton young woman's insane love quickly became a mad hatred! She became determined to wreck the happiness of this happy home, and so she poisoned John Gordon with arsenic and left his wife a widow and her innocent charge without a father. No one but Sarah Bennett could have had the motive, or the opportunity to switch the bottle containing the deadly arsenic with that containing the harmless powders regularly taken by John Gordon. It was her way of settling the score, making him pay because he would not betray his wife with her!"

This was greeted by a loud murmuring from the spectators. The Lord Chief Justice suddenly opened his eyes and the wise old face took on a scowl as he banged his gavel for order. He nodded brusquely to the prosecutor to continue and have done with dramatics.

The prosecutor's brow furrowed. "John Gordon is dead. You cannot bring him to life, much as you might wish this to be possible. But, gentlemen of the jury, you can show your sympathetic feelings to the bereaved and your solemn responsibility to society by punishing his murderess. This will serve as a solemn warning for any other young woman who might entertain similar heinous thoughts. I ask that you declare Sarah Bennett guilty!"

A hush was followed by an excited undertone of conversation among the spectators that drew the Judge's gavel and a voiced rebuke. The bewigged prosecutor took his seat with a flourish. Sarah lowered her eyes and concentrated on her folded hands, terrified that she might faint. She was anxious to retain her composure and not suggest by a sudden collapse that the prosecutor had touched on guilty nerves.

Now the thin stooped defense counsel stood up. Sarah found her mind so blurred with unpleasant thoughts that she was not able to follow his words, spoken in a nasal tone, until he was well under way. His eyes were fixed on the jury as he spoke, and he was not in any way as emotional in his appeal as the prosecutor had been.

In fact he made a point of this, saying, "I have no need to resort to the maudlin display of dramatics indulged in by my worthy opponent. I have only to remind you of the facts of the case to be sure you will not have the slightest difficulty in reaching a proper conclusion — the conclusion that my client is not guilty."

The dry, nasal voice hesitated as he

turned to stare at Sarah. Then he continued, the shrewd eyes fixed on her. "The prosecutor has given you his portrait of Sarah Bennett, one as highly colored and unrealistic as his verbiage. In short, a portrait painted by the distorted strokes of his brush as seen through his warped eyes." The elderly defense now had his opportunity of indicating her with a gesture of his thin, palsied hand. "Fortunately we do not need his painting of the accused in this courtroom because we have the lovely original here! I ask you to study her carefully, gentlemen of the jury, and then ask yourselves if this demure young woman could possibly be guilty of the crime which the prosecutor blindly demands you assign to her!"

The old lawyer paused for his own spell of hoarse coughing, and again this brought a response from the room in the way of assorted noises. He quickly resumed: "Here we have a lovely, innocent maiden of twenty-one, forced by the most tragic circumstances to leave her native England and come to Scotland. Her parents had been carried away by a swift and fatal fever, and she found herself orphaned and without money or friends. On the advice of the family doctor she came to Glasgow to seek out her father's cousin, a spinster of uncertain health. Alas, when she arrived in the strange city she was to discover that this woman had passed on several years before. So she found herself alone and without means of support."

He hesitated slightly and now gave all his attention to the jury. "Scotland was not completely inhospitable to her. A kind-hearted minister found her a position as nurse in the Gordon home. Now this man of God could not guess what tragic events would follow, nor did he know of the twisted state of affairs in that dark household. But Sarah Bennett was soon to discover that this was not the happy home the prosecutor has pictured. She loved the little child she was engaged to care for; and, as I have demonstrated, the child returned the affection. But not so the mother! Amelia Gordon had long been madly possessive and jealous toward her husband. This is a fact, proven in this courtroom by the testimony of those who had known them both for a long period. To further inflame Amelia Gordon's jealousy, her husband, troubled by her possessiveness, was cooling toward her."

The lawyer pointed a finger at the jury. "Now picture this situation as Sarah

Bennett, unaware, becomes a member of the household. Almost from the beginning she was the hapless victim of a round of recriminations between Amelia Gordon and her husband. The unhappy man did apologize to the poor girl and confess his inability to check Amelia's unrestrained jealousy. Like many men faced with an impossible situation, John Gordon sought an escape. For some men the means of escape is illicit romance; for others, alcohol; but for this victim of a woman's cruelty, it was drugs. For several years John Gordon had been dosing himself with various pills and potions under the guise that his health was failing and he needed medicine. The fact — and again I stress I am concentrating on facts only — was that he had become a hypochondriac and was consuming himself with a variety of medicines he did not need."

He paused to let the jury absorb this important information, then resumed: "John Gordon became a familiar figure at the apothecary's when his doctor refused to prescribe additional needless drugs for him. This unhappy man made no secret of the fact he was now engaged in self-medication. He would buy anything available and test it on himself. Hardly an

16

apothecary in Glasgow he did not plague for information and drugs at one time or another. His room was a clutter of bottles containing powders, liquids, and pills. Is it any surprise that arsenic also came to be among them? Or that perhaps this wretched man should contemplate suicide? I will not theorize, like the prosecution, to suggest that his wife, Amelia, might have considered poisoning her husband in a period of excessive jealousy. Instead, I shall continue to stay with the facts. I shall say that either through intent or by mistake John Gordon administered this arsenic to himself, and his death was a result of the tragic incident. That is the fact. To accuse this innocent young woman of the crime is to perpetuate the jealous fixation of a misguided wife, to ask that Sarah Bennett pay a terrible price because she happens to be young and beautiful, and because she found herself in a sordid situation not of her creation." The old man hesitated ever so slightly. "I ask that you find Sarah Bennett not guilty!"

Again there was murmuring as the defense rested his case, and with a nod in her direction, sat down.

Now the Lord Chief Justice sat erect and in a pleasant voice gave instructions to the jury. His summing up was admirably reasoned and scrupulously fair; he warned the jury about the difference between inference and proof. He pointed out: "It is for you to decide how John Gordon came by the poison, whether by his own hand, the accused's or another's. You must not rely on inference; you must be most cautious in arriving at your decision."

The jury listened with solemn faces. The twelve men selected impartially to decide her fate did not strike Sarah as the type to take long to make up their minds. She had an idea their decision would come swiftly; and after the showy performance of the prosecutor, she thought, it was not apt to be in her favor.

She was escorted to the small cell-like room in the rear to wait under the surveillance of Mrs. Bell, the stout reticent matron of Edinburgh Prison. In the bleak silence of the whitewashed room she tried to comfort herself with the memory of the concerned handsome face of the blond man. She wondered who he was, and why he had so faithfully attended her trial.

Turning to the tight-lipped matron, she asked, "Do you expect they'll be out long?"

"Most Scots' juries hae no trouble coming to a decision," the matron said,

18

taking the opportunity to record another opinion of her native heath's superiority to the England from which Sarah had come.

"This is the worst part of all," Sarah said. "This waiting to hear!"

"No doubt." The matron hunched in her chair.

Sarah looked at the formidable woman. "This must all be very familiar to you. I never even attended a trial before."

"Aye, 'tis familiar enough," the massive woman said stiffly.

Sarah found it impossible to penetrate the cold shell of the matron. She had an idea the woman was convinced of her guilt and suspicious of her every friendly overture.

Now Sarah said, "I believe the Judge to be a kindly man. I thought his instructions to the jury most fair and wise."

The matron sniffed. "He is wise enough. 'Tis his fortieth year on the bench."

Sarah was trembling again in spite of her fight to retain composure. The long days of the trial had taken their toll, and she was starting to show its effect on her.

"Might I have some tea?" she asked.

The matron gave her a hard look, then rose. "I'll call the guard and see."

The tea was brought, and Sarah found

some small comfort in its warmth and bitter strength. Then the waiting continued under the relentlessly cold eyes of Mrs. Bell.

After what seemed an eternity, but which was only a little more than an hour, the guard came to the door with an urgent air. "Jury is coming in," he announced. "Time to get her back to the courtroom."

Sarah's heart was pounding wildly, and her head was so dizzied by emotion she was hardly aware of her surroundings or what was happening. She stood before the jury as the judge requested them to give their verdict.

The lanky red-haired foreman rose, and in a solemn tone announced: "We find the charge against the defendant not proven!"

There was a wild burst of applause from the spectators, who surprisingly seemed to be on her side. Sarah clutched the rail in front of her, palms wet with perspiration, and stared out at the blur of faces. She turned and saw that the blond man had risen to applaud the verdict. And then she gave way to the impulse she had been fighting all the long days of her torture and slumped to the floor in a faint.

When she came to she was back in the whitewashed room, stretched out on the plain narrow cot, and standing around her were the matron, a guard, and an old man with a kindly, wrinkled face. It took her a moment to recognize him without his wig and robes.

The judge addressed her in a friendly tone, saying, "You need not worry yourself anymore, my dear. You are free to go where you please. With your permission, Mrs. Bell will help you change your attire for the street, and I would like to have you come home with me."

She looked up at him and in a small voice said, "That is most generous of you."

"Pshaw!" he protested. "I would be remiss in my duty if I did not take some interest in you and your fate. It is not enough to free you of the charge and turn you out into the street."

"Thank you," she said, and struggled to a sitting position. "It was foolish of me to faint. But I'm feeling more myself again."

The elderly judge gave an assenting nod of his almost completely bald head. "It was quite understandable under the circumstances."

She stared at him. "Was I really declared not guilty?"

A cynical expression was on his face as he said, "The verdict was not proven. But as the prosecution presented such a strong front, I think we may be well satisfied with that. I will wait outside while Mrs. Bell assists you in changing." With a bow the old man left the room.

Mrs. Bell, acting as if she had been denied seeing justice done, grimly helped her change into a black dress, cloak, and bonnet with a long black veil. The big woman then packed the brown dress and bonnet into the valise that held all Sarah Bennett's other worldly goods, and stood back with her customary cold expression.

Sarah felt she should express her thanks to the matron, even though the woman had shown hostility toward her. With a faltering smile, she said, "I do thank you for the kindness shown me, Mrs. Bell."

"I hae my job and I do it," the matron said obdurately.

"Thank you, anyway," Sarah told her as she picked up the heavy valise.

Mrs. Bell's broad face wore a grim look. "You may well thank your stars that you hae a bonny face and the jurors were all a daft lot of males."

Sarah said nothing to this, but made her way out of the small room knowing that Mrs. Bell had not budged in her conviction that she was a murderess. And she wondered how many others felt the same way? True, the spectators had been loud in their cheers and applause; but what had that meant? To most of them it had simply been an entertainment, and they applauded at the conclusion as they might have at the finish of a cockfight or a round of bearbaiting. It was all the same to them.

Probably many of those who had cheered the loudest at the news of her being freed were now jesting in the cobblestoned streets about her certain guilt. It was a frightening thought but one she knew she must consider. The verdict "not proven" had given her her freedom, but a freedom sadly lacking in honor. Perhaps a few in the courtroom believed in her — the blond man who had been so faithful in his attendance and so sympathetic in his glances, for one; certainly the judge, for another. But probably her supporters could be counted on the fingers of one hand. How fortunate she was that the judge had elected to show an interest in her.

The old man was waiting for her in the corridor, with a guard at his side. As soon as she appeared he told the guard, "Take her bag, my good fellow, and escort us to my carriage." The old man gently took her arm. "You are no longer feeling faint, I trust?"

Studying him from behind her veil, she managed a forlorn smile, "No. I'm feeling much better, thank you."

They left the courthouse by a rear exit to avoid any curiosity seekers, and the judge assisted her into his modest single-horse carriage, then got in beside her. The guard put her valise on the floor by her feet and closed the door. The driver cracked his whip and they rattled off down the cobbled side street.

The judge gave her a pleasant smile. "I fear you have had a bad time during your stay in Scotland. I hope to prove to you that we are all not savages in this northern country of ours."

"I am well aware of that," she said sincerely. "What happened to me here could have happened anywhere."

"I hope you will remember that," the judge said earnestly. "It would be a grave error to let you fend for yourself at this time. There are unscrupulous persons who have undoubtedly been watching the trial, and aware of your beauty and helpless position, they would attempt to ingratiate themselves with you and use you for their own wicked purposes."

"Yes," she said faintly.

"That is why I am taking you to my home today," the judge explained, "and why I shall concern myself with your future."

"Truly there is no one else to worry about it," she said.

"Then allow a crusty old bachelor to do what little he may," he said with a chuckle. "I have a most excellent cook and housekeeper, and she is at this very moment preparing a good meal for our arrival. I find trials give me a most monstrous appetite!"

"I have been able to eat little these past few weeks," she admitted.

"You must begin doing better right away," the judge said. And pointing out the side window of the carriage, he continued, "This is High Street, and yonder is the Tron Church. Not old as age is understood in Auld Reekie, our sentimental nickname for this old town of Edinburgh, but built in 1647. During the great fire that swept the largest part of High Street when I was a boy its steeple collapsed. But it's long since been restored, and this is the central gathering spot to celebrate the new year."

Sarah peered out and got as clear a view as her veil would allow. The Tron showed four clocks, one on each side of its steeple.

It was not a handsome building, with its Presbyterian dourness.

The judge was speaking again. "Now there is St. Giles, the most famous of all our churches. John Knox preached there, and it was there that Jenny Geddes threw a stool at the head of the dean who attempted to read the order of worship instituted by command of Charles the First. And farther down we have the house where John Knox lived, and around the corner is St. Celia's Hall."

Sarah watched with more interest than her upset condition warranted, knowing that he was showing her these places in an attempt to take her mind off herself. The least she could do was to try and play her part.

He went on telling her about the romantic old city with the newer section, now a hundred years old, boasting many wide straight streets, fine shops, famous restaurants, and impressive public buildings. Sarah was fascinated by her glimpse of the castle and the steep, narrow lanes that they now traversed on their way to the judge's neat little stone house.

A buxom, smiling woman, who was introduced as Mrs. MacPherson, opened the door to them. And soon Sarah was at her ease in a small parlor, clean and shining, sporting prints on the walls, the round table set with blue plates, narrow silver knives and forks, scones, a loaf of black bread, rich yellow butter, a jug of cream.

The judge gave her a glass of sherry and helped himself from a decanter of whisky. Then standing by her with glass in hand, he smiled and said, "We are to have a guest. So enjoy your aperitif while we await him."

Sarah sipped her sherry and found it took away some of the faint, nervous feeling. "I cannot continue to impose on you," she said.

"Pray do not think of it in that way," the old jurist implored her. "I do not consider my duties at an end when I remove my wig and robes."

"I do not know just how I will go about seeking employment," Sarah confessed. "So much scandal was created by the trial, I fear it will follow me wherever I go. Even to my native England."

The judge nodded. "I know your problem, my dear. It seems to me you require employment in some quiet area until all the talk subsides. The public has a notably short memory, and within a year or two you should be able to move about freely."

"I am comforted by your words," she said, with a small smile. "But that blessed time seems so far off."

"I quite understand." The judge's wrinkled face showed his concern. "But you will be heartened to know that the son of a dear friend of mine has come forward with just such an offer for you."

Sarah felt her spirits rise for the first time since the beginning of the trial. "You really mean it?"

"Indeed I do!" The judge drained his whisky glass with satisfaction. "This young man has known bitter tragedy almost the equal of yours. He has a fine old estate in a village called Rawlwyn on the outskirts of this city. His mansion, Dankhurst, was built by his maternal grandfather, Stephen Dank, some seventy years ago. The young man's name is John Stone, and when I approached him on your behalf he was most ready to offer help."

"Then his good heart must equal your own," Sarah said impulsively.

The judge smiled. "John Stone is a fine person. But as I have told you, he also has known tragedy. His wife died after a sad period of failing health of some wasting disease the family doctor could not diagnose or cope with. He was left to raise his seven-year-old son alone. Luckily he was able to call on his wife's cousin to look after his household affairs; she had already been on the scene as nurse and companion to his failing wife. His half brother, Rodney Stone — one of our more promising poets, of whom you may have heard — also lives at Dankhurst."

"I am not familiar with his work," Sarah confessed.

"His fame is growing," the judge assured her. "There was also a half sister, Justine, but she died shortly after John's marriage under the saddest of circumstances — victim of a fire in a cottage she and her husband occupied in France. She was extremely fond of John and, I must confess, showed an undue resentment when he married."

"But you say she was herself married?"

"That happened after John took a wife. Very shortly afterward. In a pique, the girl eloped to France with a man she'd met only a few weeks before. John was most distressed at the estrangement between himself and Justine, and the shock of her violent death did his health no good."

"Still, I assume he is well now?" Sarah ventured.

The jurist frowned slightly. "Not as well

as I would like. There is a strange brooding about him. His mental state veers on the melancholy. The second tragedy — his wife's mysterious illness and eventual death — plunged him into a state of moody apathy. I have not visited Dankhurst lately, but I have heard rumors that he has not been looking after it as he should. Instead, he spends most of his time these days on his hobby of research into ancient Egyptian writings. He took honors in this subject at Oxford and has contributed to the field over the years. So he lives on his inherited wealth and tenant rents, and takes little interest in improving his ancestral mansion or keeping up the grounds. I also worry that the little boy may suffer neglect. I refer, of course, to a neglect of love and affection only. That is why I was delighted when John suggested that you might go to Dankhurst as the lad's governess."

Sarah sighed. "It is a wonder that I am invited to work in any respectable home."

"No worry about that," the judge said. "John Stone is sympathetic to your plight. One of his own ancestors was involved in a poisoning case, and she took her life as a result. John believes she was innocent having made a study of the history of the case. This has led him to a deep interest in poisoners and poisonings. He is a man of great intellect and humanity."

"I am sure he must be," she said, putting down her empty sherry glass.

From the outer hallway a bell rang. The judge said, "That must be John Stone now," and he moved to the doorway to greet him.

Sarah sat very erect in her chair, feeling nervous all over again as she heard the bluff Mrs. MacPherson greet the new guest. Then the judge hailed him heartily by name, and a moment later Sarah had her first glimpse of her new employer as he entered the parlor.

She gave a startled gasp, for he proved to be none other than the handsome, serious-faced blond man who had attended her trial.

2

The young man's face brightened as the judge introduced him to Sarah. He came across, and taking her hand, said, "What a privilege to at last be able to offer you my sympathy and congratulations."

She smiled at him demurely. "I must confess to already being conscious of your sympathy for me, since I noted your presence in the courtroom day after day."

John Stone nodded, his blue eyes fixed on hers. "It is true. I have remained in Edinburgh for the full term of your trial. I can only suggest the jury were clod-heads not to have given you a true verdict of not guilty. But at least you have your freedom."

"Which is all that I consider important," the judge intervened.

John Stone gave his attention to the older man. "But the charge against her was so unjust as to constitute a libel. Anyone need only look at Miss Bennett to know she is not capable of murder."

"Well, let that pass," the judge said easily. "I have been happy to inform her of your offer."

John Stone looked her way again. "I trust you will give it consideration."

"Indeed I am grateful to you for the invitation to join your household," she said. "I shall be happy to take charge of your son."

"Young Richard is a frail lad," John Stone said with a sigh. "I fear he has inherited his delicate nature from his mother. But he has a lively mind, and I'm sure you will be drawn to him."

"When do you plan to return to Dankhurst?" the judge asked.

"I should like to leave early in the morning," John Stone said. "I've been in the city since Miss Bennett's trial began, except for last weekend, and so I have let my affairs get behind. I'm anxious not to lose further time." He looked Sarah's way. "Would you be ready to leave early tomorrow?"

"At any time," she assured him.

Seeing John Stone at close range, Sarah was aware that he was even more impressively handsome than she had judged him in the courtroom. He was slim and elegant in a carefully cut gray suit with a gray silk cravat to match. His pallor was more noticeable now, and there was a melancholy air about him. He seldom smiled, although he was pleasant enough.

She put down his sober mien to the severe misfortune he had suffered. She could count herself lucky that because of the long-ago tragedy in his own family he had a special interest in anyone involved in a poisoning case. The air of aloof gloom that cloaked him could be put down to the loss of his beloved wife and the violent death of his sister. Sarah hoped the future might hold better things for John Stone; he had already experienced so much unhappiness.

There was no reluctance on her part to accept his offer of employment. She knew that John Stone's fine mansion would hold none of the hazards for her that she had faced with the Gordons. It meant an ideal chance to get a much-needed fresh start.

The judge spoke up: "Then you shall dine with us, John. Miss Bennett will spend the night here, and in the morning I shall drive her to the railway station in my carriage."

"That will be excellent, sir," John Stone said in his grave fashion.

And so they sat down to the fine dinner Mrs. MacPherson had readied for them. Afterward the men lingered at the table over brandy and cigars. Sarah was greatly stirred by John Stone's erudition and eloquence. He talked to her and the judge of the glories of ancient Egypt, his blue eyes bright with enthusiasm. It was clear he was an authority on the subject.

Once he paused to look at her across the table, and said, "Back in those early days of civilization there was much more sophistication than we can guess. As an example, the Egyptians had developed the science of poisoning to a fine art. Through the ages we have forgotten and lost many of their more subtle methods."

"Indeed!" she had said with mild wonder, somewhat dismayed that he should speak of such matters in view of her recent plight.

He must have noted the distress in her face, because he quickly apologized. "I fear I have upset you with my thoughtless remark."

"It's quite all right," she assured him, and glanced down at her plate.

The judge at once intervened. "I know you meant no harm, John," he told the young man. "And you are quite right. The Egyptians were masters of the art of poisoning. A fascinating aspect of ancient crime."

"I have lately been immersing myself in

Egyptian lore," the young man confessed. "It has taught me much, and I have been able to free myself from the unhappy present."

The judge frowned and shook his head. "You are too young to seek such solace. You should be involved with the daily life around you. Otherwise you will wither in mind and body and find yourself old before your time."

"Good advice, sir," the young man said. "I only wish I had the strength to follow it."

"You must, if only for the sake of your boy," the judge told him.

John Stone nodded gravely. "Yes, I must forget this pitying of myself and give more thought to him." He looked Sarah's way again. "I shall look to you for serious support in this area, Miss Bennett."

She smiled. "You may be assured that I will give my best attention to your son."

The judge stifled a yawn. "Bless me," he said. "It's after nine o'clock!"

"And time for me to leave if we're to make an early departure," John Stone said, rising. He bowed to Sarah. "I shall be looking forward to seeing you again in the morning, Miss Bennett."

Mrs. MacPherson showed her up to the

modest room with the single iron-frame bed and the plain dresser. The old house-keeper placed a small lamp on the bedside table and checked the commode to see that all was in order.

"Have a good night's rest for your journey, miss," she advised Sarah, and left.

Plain though the room might be, it was a great improvement over the grim prison cell from which she'd so recently emerged. Standing there in the shadowed room, with the flickering flame of the small lamp casting an eerie reflection on the walls and ceiling, Sarah wondered if the nightmarish experience she'd gone through would ever completely leave her, or if she would be haunted the rest of her days by the sordid happenings in the Gordon household.

Such were her thoughts when she heard the creak of a floor board from the dark hallway and glanced fearfully out the still-open door to see who might be lurking there in the darkness. In a moment a figure took shape in the shadows, and she saw it was the judge.

He stood in the doorway, studying her. "You will be comfortable here?"

"Oh, yes! It is like a castle compared with what I have known these past weeks."

"It is far from a castle," the old man said

37

with a faint smile. "I'm certain your quarters will be larger and much more elaborate at Dankhurst, unless the place has gone down more than I've been told."

"We are to be at the railway station at eight?" she inquired. "I believe he said the train left at fifteen minutes after the hour."

"He did indeed," the judge agreed, and continued to hesitate there. At last, rather awkwardly, he said, "I am beginning to realize my responsibility in turning you over to this young man. I must confess I find myself with worries as to your safety."

Her eyebrows raised. "Indeed? But why?"

"No special reason," he admitted, "beyond the fact I have encouraged you to accept his employment offer. You will be a good fifteen miles outside the city and among strangers in a relatively small village."

"So much the better."

"In a sense, that is true," the judge agreed. "But you will also be isolated and alone. I want you to promise to write me at once if you are not completely at ease in your new post. Write me, and I shall take care of your return to Edinburgh."

"I promise," she told him. "But surely there can be no need for alarm? John Stone seems a man of high ideals, and his son must be a fine little boy."

"So it would seem," the judge agreed. "But life is filled with ambiguities, and it is wise to consider every possibility."

"If you'd like, I will write you a weekly letter," she suggested. "I will let you know all that is happening and have you judge the situation for yourself."

The old man nodded his approval. "Now that is an excellent suggestion," he said. "The letters will mean a great deal to me for their own value alone. And it will be a means to assure me of your continuing welfare."

"Then it is settled," she said with a smile. "Though I think we need have no fears about John Stone not being a gentle and considerate employer."

He stood silently in the shadows as she said this, and she thought his face took on the troubled expression again. "You are probably right," he said. "But I would be less than truthful if I did not tell you I noticed a sad change in him tonight. He seems to be steadily going downhill. He seems more vague, moody, and aloof than I have ever known him. In the old days he was a merry, jovial fellow with a joke always on his lips and a ready laugh. Tonight a smile did not escape from him."

"Surely it is because of all the sorrow he has known?"

"Whatever it is, I am concerned that he might conceivably have a health or nervous collapse," the judge warned her. "In which case I would not want you there. You have gone through enough as it is."

"Perhaps the trial has worn him down," she suggested. "He would have been wiser to have followed it in the penny papers."

"Let us worry no more about it," the judge said. "But keep what I've said uppermost in your thoughts, and be sure to send me a weekly account of your doings."

She again promised she would, and they exchanged good nights. She closed the door and stood alone, feeling somewhat perplexed at what the judge had just told her. She had felt he was so positive that his move would be right for her before John Stone had presented himself, and now he seemed doubtful and loath that he had so strongly recommended she take the position at Dankhurst. Had he seen something in the young man's behavior that she had missed, some warning signal that made him hesitate? It was entirely possible, for John Stone was a stranger to her, and she would not be alert to the small subtleties of his manner.

Yet she could not forget that it had been the sober blond man who had come to the courtroom every day of the trial and sustained her with the encouragement of his presence. It seemed like the fulfillment of a pleasant dream that he should turn out to be John Stone, ready to take her under his protection and into his home. She would not let the judge's worries upset her. Let her be wise enough to accept this stroke of good fortune that had come her way at last.

Thinking thus, she fell into the deep sleep of the exhausted. The strenuous day in court, capped by this meeting with John Stone, had drained her strength. And yet at some point in the night she began to dream and toss restlessly in her bed. Her pretty features twisted with fear, and small moans of distress emerged from her as she grasped the sheets with fevered hands. She was having a nightmare visit to her new home of Dankhurst, and she stood before it in the eerie world of her dream state to find it looming dark and forbidding. John Stone was at her side. He smiled a reassurance to her as he led her to the great arched oaken door and pushed it open to reveal the yawning blackness of an immense hallway. She held back, but he drew her in after him. She trembled with fear, but he continued to lead her into a giant room with a high ceiling, and in it were people sitting in chairs all around the walls. People with the gargoyle faces of the spectators at the trial!

And as she screamed with terror John Stone turned to her with a triumphant smile, the first smile she had ever seen on his serious face. And before all those assembled there he shouted, "I have brought you here for my own purpose. I am a specialist in ancient Egyptian poisons and you are a murderess who has used poison!"

In her dream, Sarah recoiled in horror at his words and began to scream wildly. She wakened to the darkness of the tiny room in the rear of the judge's stone house, still screaming. In a moment, after she had calmed a little and realized it had been an ugly nightmare she heard a scuffling in the hallway and the anxious voice of Mrs. MacPherson.

"Are you all right, miss?" came the voice from the other side of the door.

Sarah swallowed hard. "Yes," she said tensely. "I'm sorry to have disturbed you. I was having a dreadful dream."

"Yes, miss," Mrs. MacPherson sounded sympathetic and sleepy. "Is there anything I can do?"

"No. I'm sure I'll be all right now. Thank you."

It took some time for Sarah to get to sleep again, but when she did she slept right through until the housekeeper tapped at her door the next morning. From then on it was a rush and a scurry until they arrived at the pandemonium of the railway station that served Edinburgh. People hurried in every direction; porters and trainmen in uniform shouted information in harsh voices; children trailed after their parents as they made their way to the great puffing steam engines. It was all very busy, noisy, and dirty.

Sarah clutched the old judge's arm, timid of the hurly-burly surrounding them and having no idea where they would go to meet John Stone. Then she saw the tall blond man emerge from the crowds and come straight toward them.

He nodded briskly to the judge. "Thank you for getting Miss Bennett here on time, sir," he said, gray hat in hand. "We have just time to board the train." He spoke loudly in order to be heard above the din.

The judge turned to her with a kindly expression on his wrinkled face. "Remember all that I have told you, my dear. Let me hear from you."

The realization that this was a leave-taking from the first sure friend she had known since the death of her parents brought her a moment of panic. She fought hard to keep up a calm front, tears brimming in her eyes.

"How can I thank you?" she asked.

But the noise was so great her words were drowned by it, and the judge, not knowing what she had said, responded by smiling vaguely and nodding. At the same moment John Stone took her by the arm, and with a final goodby to the judge, dragged her quickly off through the milling confusion of the station.

Sarah had it in her mind to utter a protest at this unceremonious treatment, but stifled it, knowing that they probably were late for their train. John Stone had already found a compartment and stowed their luggage in it, and he now assisted her inside and closed the door. They had one seat to themselves; across from them sat two elderly women, thin and vinegary-looking, wearing musty black gowns and tiny bonnets with feathers. When she and John entered the compartment the two women exchanged knowing glances. Beside them, in a faded green-checked suit and a green bowler hat, so shabby it

44

seemed it might have moss growing on it, was a thin old man whose pinched features so much resembled those of the two women that Sarah decided he must be their brother. He had a copy of the *Illustrated London News* in his hands and he raised his eyes above it to scowl at Sarah and John, then returned to his reading.

They had no sooner seated themselves than the train gave a great lurch, there was a loud blast from the engine, and they began to move slowly forward. As the train yard and the sooty slums through which they were passing were nothing to look at, Sarah gave her attention to the young man at her side. "How long will it take us to reach Rawlwyn?" she asked.

"About an hour and a half," he said. "There are several stops along the way." He spoke as if his mind were on something else, and she saw that he looked as pale as on the previous day and infinitely more weary. Also he seemed to be avoiding the eyes of the grim-visaged trio sitting across from them, who were avidly taking in every word.

Feeling self-conscious, Sarah attempted a smile as she said, "It's a pleasant day. I'm sure it will be a nice journey once we leave this section of the city."

John Stone sighed. "I fear the scenery is

of the undistinguished rural variety. Not until we reach Rawlwyn can you see any large mountains in the background. This countryside may remind you of parts of England."

And so it did, Sarah decided, as she stared absently out the window at the passing meadows, hills, and tiny rivers, with small farms dotted like toy buildings here and there. It was not long before they came to the first station, a modest one-story building with a platform and a board at roof-level, with its name painted on it. John Stone took advantage of the brief stop to step onto the platform and stretch his legs. Sarah was worried that he might not return in time and thus miss the train. Also she could not help overhearing a whispered conversation going on among the three opposite her.

The green bowler leaned toward the two women and in a whisky whisper said, "Looks as if John Stone is starting all over again!"

"The brazen nerve of it! After what happened to poor dear Penelope!"

"He should have been punished, and he would have if he hadn't had old Dr. Gideon to back him up!" the other woman whispered, and pursed her lips.

"I wouldn't want to be in this one's shoes," the man said. "She's liable to wind up suffering from the same lingering disease Penelope had." He went back to his magazine as John Stone opened the door, swung lightly up into the compartment again, and resumed his seat beside her.

Ignoring the glares of the two women in black, Sarah asked him, "Will somebody be at the train to meet us?"

"My half-brother, Rodney," John Stone said. "He will bring the rig."

"He is the poet?"

"He plays at it," John said stiffly. "He could be successful if he gave his attention to it properly, but he is not so disposed."

Sarah hesitated to ask any more questions. She had no wish to supply the trio opposite with gossip. She knew John was acquainted with them, and they knew him well enough, yet they did not speak. And she had been shocked by their whisperings. She did not know what their references to the dead Penelope meant, but she was embarrassed at the knowledge that they were convinced John Stone was bringing her to Dankhurst to become his second bride. Feeling ill at ease, she tried to cover her upset by continuing to stare out at the passing countryside.

It was with relief that she saw that the station at which they were halting was Rawlwyn. The trio across from them were on their feet and busy gathering their baggage, with much argument and complaining. John, white-faced and coldly composed, stood with his bag in one hand and her valise in the other. When the train came to a full halt he was the first out, and helped her down onto the platform. Their three traveling companions began emerging as she and John walked along the wooden platform.

Sarah recognized Rodney Stone before John had a chance to point him out to her. The tall, dark-haired man came striding down the platform to meet them, his smiling face not quite as handsome as John's, but resembling John to a remarkable degree. But in Rodney's face there was a touch of weakness. He wore corduroy trousers and a tweed jacket, his white shirt was open at the neck, and he was hatless. He had a swaggering, romantic air about him.

Coming up to them he offered a mocking bow and said, "What a proper looking pair you two make!" His voice had a musical lilt.

John Stone looked angry. "We can do

without your dramatics, Rod," he snapped. "My half-brother, Rodney, Miss Bennett. This is Miss Sarah Bennett, who has come to take care of Richard, as you know."

Rodney shook Sarah's hand. "It's a true pleasure to welcome you to this drap part of the world, Miss Bennett. If we had a few more visitors like yourself, I'd find it more bearable."

John glanced back at the trio who'd shared the compartment with them, and who were now approaching. In a low voice he warned Rod, "Do without the fancy words. The Regan sisters and their brother Tom are coming this way. We've had the misfortune of sharing a compartment with them all the way down, and I can do without having to see them again."

"They are a sorry group," Rodney agreed with a twinkle in his black eyes. Taking up Sarah's valise and starting to lead them from the platform to the waiting rig, he added, "They could serve in the witches' scene from *Macbeth* any day."

With Rodney at the reins and their bags stowed safely aboard, Sarah and John sat side by side in the jogging little cart as it wound its way through pleasant country lanes to their destination.

John gave her a glance. "I hope those

three didn't bother you in any way," he said. "Did they address themselves to you when I was out of the compartment?"

"No," she said. "Though they did whisper among themselves."

"Village gossips!" he said angrily. "They are not my friends. Many of the village people resent us. We own a great many farms and some of the houses in the village. Landlords are rarely popular with their tenants."

"So I have heard," she agreed, privately wondering if that was all that had caused the rift between John and the villagers.

"You must close your ears to any scandal you may hear in the village," he went on. "In any event, you will seldom leave Dankhurst."

Although she was later to have concern about this, it did not cause her any misgivings at the time. She was quite willing to bury herself in this rather remote countryside until she was forgotten and could again take her place in the world without the ugliness of her past shadowing her.

They traveled up a rather steep section of road, and John pointed out a blue mountain far to the left with a peak of white snow. When they arrived at the entrance to Dankhurst the high iron gates, attached to brick pillars, were open. A dark metal plate engraved with *Dankhurst* was mounted on each of the pillars. Tall evergreens fenced the estate and bordered the roadway to the house.

After a few minutes they came out into the open and there, straight ahead, was the old mansion — a sprawling stone building, four stories high, with a mansard roof. There were deep porches, tall French windows, massive cornices, and sweeping roofs topped by iron cresting. The house had striking power and dignity, but also an air of neglect. The grounds themselves looked badly in need of maintenance.

Although the lawns had been kept mowed, the shrubbery was unkempt and running wild. A large fountain to the right of the entrance was no longer in working condition, and its dark center iron work showed white bird droppings; the water in the shallow, circular pool surrounding the fountain was stagnant, green, and evil-looking, with a scattering of leaves on its surface. Some grayish statuary, placed about the lawn, had a grim abandoned air. Pervading the whole place was a forbidding atmosphere that made Sarah recall her nightmare.

"Well, how do you like it?" John Stone

asked as the rig halted before the porch.

"It's so large," she said awkwardly. "And so impressive."

John sighed as he glanced about at the bedraggled lawn. "I could be accused of neglecting my duties," he admitted. "I have had no interest in the place lately."

Rodney Stone had already jumped down and was removing the bags and placing them on the gravel driveway. He stood by to assist Sarah next, and as he took her hand in his to balance her he said, with a mocking smile, "Welcome to Castle Grim, dear Miss Bennett. I'm sure you're already apprehensive of it."

"Not really," she said, thinking that he was truly a rather nice young man in spite of his bitter humor.

John, on the ground at her side, murmured, "Why must you indulge in these dubious pleasantries, Rod? Aren't you satisfied that we have enough problems?"

Rodney bowed. "Forgive me, John. I have no proper sense of aptness."

They mounted the porch steps and approached the broad oaken door, which swung open to reveal an attractive young woman in a yellow dress with fancy trim. She had an aristocratic face with a high forehead, and her brown hair was plaited and coiled in braids at the base of her neck. Her brown eyes were widely spaced and her smile was pleasant.

In a soft voice, she said, "Welcome to Dankhurst, Miss Bennett. I am Abigail Durmot."

"Thank you," Sarah said. So this was the cousin who had come to the old mansion to nurse Penelope and who remained as housekeeper for John Stone after his wife's death. She appeared attractive and young enough to make him a most suitable wife, Sarah thought.

"How is Richard?" John asked. "Why isn't he here to greet Miss Bennett?"

Abigail looked uneasy. "I am truly sorry," she said. "But the boy came down with one of his fever attacks last night. I was forced to summon Dr. Gideon, and he insisted the boy must remain in bed for a few days." She turned to Sarah, adding, "I regret that your new charge does not have robust health."

John frowned. "He does well enough, except for these feverish spells. I agree with the doctor that he will grow out of them. No harm done in any event. It will give Miss Bennett time to feel comfortable here before she meets him."

"That is so," Abigail agreed, and gave

53

another of her engaging smiles.

Rodney Stone, who had vanished upstairs with the bags, now returned, and stopping by John, said, "I have placed Miss Bennett's valise in the front bedroom on the third floor. That is where Abigail said she would be staying."

John nodded. "Thank you. I'll show Miss Bennett upstairs."

Rodney bowed to her with a mocking light in his mischievous black eyes, and she felt certain she was going to be friends with this dark, curly-haired young man. Then she followed John Stone up the broad staircase leading to the second floor. A second flight, slightly steeper, led to the third floor.

Escorting her down the corridor, John Stone explained, "We are only using three floors of the house at the moment. The fourth is quite deserted, used only for storage. Most of the bedrooms are on this floor, and here is yours."

He opened a door on the right and she found herself in a pleasant room with corner windows that had lace curtains and dark red drapes. A fireplace in red brick contrasted with the white walls and woodwork, and the ample four-poster bed looked most comfortable. A dresser, a washstand, some assorted chairs, and a red carpet completed the furnishings of the large room. The judge had been right. It was more luxurious than any she'd ever known.

"It's wonderful!" she exclaimed, and noted that Rodney had left her valise on a plain chair near the dresser.

John moved to a window. "This overlooks the garden and is almost directly above the fountain and lily pond. The fountain no longer works, and the lily pond receives no care. But at least you do have a view of them."

"You are much too kind," she said. "And I would like to see your son."

"Later," he said, his expression grave. "There is no need to rush things. He is not well. When you are settled come down and take a look around the place."

"Thank you, I will," she promised. She hesitated a moment, feeling awkward about the next question she must ask. Finally she said, "Do they know about me here?"

John Stone looked solemn. "Only Abigail and Rodney," he said. "I had to tell them. They would have found out for themselves, since they both read the Edinburgh paper and knew I was attending the trial. Neither my son nor the servants know about you."

"It's just that I want to know my position here," she said.

"Quite understandable," John agreed. "And I hope you will be happy with us." He then left her, and she began to unpack.

It was fully a half hour later when she went down to take a stroll in the garden. She walked a distance from the house to stand back and study it. She saw that most of the windows on the top floor had closed shutters. And she was amazed at the number of chimneys the old house had. More than a dozen!

"Counting the chimneys?" a cheerful voice asked from behind her.

She turned to see a smiling Rodney. "We have a total of seventeen chimneys and seventeen fireplaces. It takes a deal of wood during a cold winter."

"I can imagine," she said.

His eyes met hers. "So you came up on the train with the terrible Regans. Did they say anything to you behind John's back? If so, you must have found it ironical. You see, they, along with other villagers, believe that John poisoned his wife."

3

The young poet's casual statement was all the more shattering because it was so completely unexpected. Sarah stared at his smiling face, wondering if she had heard him correctly. But she knew she had. Standing in the warm noon sunshine she felt a chill. Had she escaped from one nightmare only to find herself trapped in another? Could it be that the judge's sudden doubts about John Stone were well-founded?

She said, "I'm not sure I understand."

"I should think you'd be familiar enough with poison and poisoners," Rodney said with a mocking tone. "You are *the* Sarah Bennett, aren't you?"

"Yes," she said faintly. "But what is this about your brother?"

"You had your experience with a jealous woman and the law," Rodney said. "My brother is being accused of a crime by people who should know better — the very villagers whom he has so often befriended.

But they are jealous of his wealth and generally a suspicious lot. So when Penelope died of that mysterious ailment they began gossiping about how John had poisoned her so he could make Abigail his wife. And they claim that old Thaddeus Gideon was in on it. He's an ancient doctor, in disfavor with the village because of his advanced age, who is still our family doctor."

"But why does your brother allow them to say such things?"

"What can he do? In the end he decided to ignore the whole thing. It's too ridiculous! Everyone knows the sort of man John is, that he truly loved Penelope. Her death has made a saddened, changed man of him. I can vouch for that. And I vow Abigail has eyes more for me than for my sober brother. Dr. Gideon may be in his dotage, but he is honest and not as weak in the head as the villagers maintain. So you see, Miss Bennett, it is all merely a storm in a teacup. No one thought to make charges against my brother as they did against you. And any such charge would be just as much in error as was the one against you. Yet all this served a purpose."

"Indeed?"

He smiled at her knowingly. "And an excellent one I might say. It brought about his interest in you and your trial. And his knowledge of the unfair accusations against him made him sympathetic to you."

"I had no idea."

"He probably felt it wiser not to mention it."

"I knew those people in the railway carriage were whispering peculiar things about him," Sarah recalled. "But I had no idea they were accusing him of being a murderer."

"I felt you were entitled to know the facts," Rodney told her, "before you heard some distorted version from someone in the village."

"The judge mentioned his wife's death and the tragic fate his sister met some years ago."

Rodney at once looked concerned. "It's all right for you to mention Penelope, but never say anything about Justine. Even though it happened some time ago, he still feels dreadfully guilty about her being burned to death."

"But that is very unfair to himself!"

"Justine was my full sister," Rodney said, "and I have tried to make him see that her possessive jealousy concerning him was unnatural. Her fleeing to France with that man, and her subsequent death resulted from that madness and not through any fault of his." He shrugged. "But you know what a strange sort of person John is. How deeply he feels things."

"I sympathize with him," she said.

"Don't let your sympathy rule your mind," Rodney warned. "John is mostly to blame for his unhappiness, as you will discover. And his moodiness is most upsetting to young Richard's health, that and the boy's yearning for his mother."

"I am anxious to see him," she said. "But Mr. Stone felt there was no hurry. He was afraid I'd disturb the boy."

"He avoids Richard on the one hand," Rodney complained, "and is too protective of him on the other."

"Thank you for your frankness," Sarah said. "It will make things easier for me."

"Richard needs a woman's care and love," Rodney said, looking up at the house. "Abigail is busy with the running of the household and is not overfond of children in any case. I think you are badly needed here and will do a good job."

"What of these fevers?"

"The boy has weak lungs. It is in his mother's family. I have seen him spit blood. These fever bouts are part of it. Unless he has excellent care I fear that John will suffer yet another bereavement."

Sarah showed concern. "That mustn't happen!"

"I trust that it doesn't. Richard is a sweet lad." He tapped an alabaster replica of a woman in a typical gown of the period. The statuary had turned a dirty gray, and the nose was chipped off by some random blow. "My grandfather had a strange idea of art. That is why he dotted the grounds with what were contemporary figures of his day. John and I feel they are monstrosities, but we hate to have them taken away."

She regarded the full-size figure and the others within view. "They must have an eerie appearance at night."

He laughed. "They do help to build the legend that the house is haunted. You are no doubt familiar with the legend of Priscilla Kirk?"

"Yes. The judge spoke to me of her. She was one of your ancestors, who killed herself because of a false murder charge, wasn't she?"

"Indeed she was," he agreed. "According to the portrait which you must see in the living room, she was a rare beauty. She feared being turned over to the authorities, although she was innocent. Despairing of proving her innocence, she drowned herself."

Sarah said pointedly, "Wasn't she also accused falsely of a poisoning?"

"True. You have come to the right spot. She threw herself in the river, so the legend goes. And she has since stalked Dankhurst on certain dark nights. I tell you, few of the villagers will come within a distance of the estate after sunset. And we have no poachers. So I say the legend and the statues that look like ghostly figures have done a good job."

She smiled at him. "And you are the poet."

"John would tell you the profligate. He does not approve of my attitude toward life any more than I do his."

"He said as much to me," she admitted.

The curly-haired Rodney gave her an amused look. "The truth is that I am not a good poet, and to avoid admitting that I have a feeble talent, I waste a good deal of my time on wine and women, neglecting the song."

"In this land of Robert Burns I should think the ambition to be a poet would be strong in one of talent. And when you are reputed to have such rich talents, is it not a shame to waste them?"

He laughed and quoted: "This is my heath, the land that is mine,/where first I

62

drew breath and will end my time./And those who here lived, and those who here died/were of my same flesh and of my same pride."

"Thank you," she said politely.

"It's poor stuff and you know it," he said. "But my head is full of it. I think myself lucky to have an independent income and to be able to share this old house with John. And should anything happen to John, and should Richard not live to take over, I would be the solitary owner of this gloomy estate."

She offered a startled little laugh. "That is not apt to happen."

"It is not to be expected," he corrected her. "But sometimes things happen that we least expect." He paused. "But I am taking too much of your time."

"Quite the contrary," Sarah insisted. "You are offering a picture of Scottish life quite revealing to me. When I first came north I looked for a land of savages in kilts, the wild laments of bagpipes, and Highland dancers in full regalia."

"And you have seen little of such things?"

"I'm afraid that is so."

"You will find none of them at Dankhurst," Rodney said. "We come from a mixture of stock in which English blood

63

prevails. And so on this estate the Scottish customs and pageantry are indulged in only in a most moderate fashion."

"I see."

"But all around us the traditions are celebrated," Rodney went on. "And I will make sure you attend at least one Highland gathering — an experience you will not be likely to forget. Meanwhile you must settle down to our bleak existence here."

"I look forward to it."

Rodney Stone gave her a teasing smile. "And the ghost of Priscilla Kirk?"

"I am not as impressionable as your villagers," she promised. "It will take more than the recounting of a legend and some gray statues under the moonlight to make me see phantoms."

"Bravely spoken!" Rodney said mockingly. "But we shall see."

"At least you have warned me."

"And now I must be off," he said, with a glance toward the house. "I see my brother on his way to join us, and he has an ugly glint in his eye. It might be that he thinks I'm forcing myself on you."

"I'll straighten him out on that point," she promised.

"Pray do," Rodney said. "At any rate, I

find him a dreary fellow and will wander off to avoid his rebukes." He gave her another of his mocking smiles and hurried toward a path leading to the rear of the mansion.

The blond young master of Dankhurst came striding over to her with a severe expression on his handsome face. Wearing the same gray suit in which he had journeyed from Edinburgh, he looked every inch the country squire.

"I trust Rodney was not annoying you with some of his nonsensical talk," he said.

"Not at all. I find him amusing."

John gazed sternly at the retreating figure of his brother. "I must warn you that he is irresponsible in both speech and habits. And can be charming as well, which makes him truly dangerous."

"Perhaps his idleness serves to lead him into temptation," she suggested. "Does he do nothing with his days but compose occasional verse?"

"Very little else," John said, glancing at her again. "Often he goes to the village or even as far as Edinburgh, and does not return for a week or more. He seems to take a special enjoyment in low companions on such occasions."

It was plain that John Stone's disapproval of Rodney was strong and there was little likelihood of his changing his mind about him. Sarah decided she could best serve the cause of harmony in the old house by infrequent mention of Rodney in John's presence. With this in mind, she glanced toward the gray-stone mansion and prepared to discuss it.

"Your home has a noble air," she said. "A true dignity."

John followed her glance. "I am much attached to it," he acknowledged, "although there are those who dub it bleak."

"I do not see it that way," she said.

"I haven't shown you the interior, beyond taking you to your room," John said. "If you will accompany me now, I have some spare time before lunch and would be happy to give you a short tour of its principal rooms."

"Thank you," she said. And they began to stroll back toward the old house.

"I am most anxious to make the acquaintance of my charge," Sarah admitted as they walked over the short-cropped grass.

John's head was bent forward slightly. "After lunch," he said.

"Is the boy well advanced in his studies?"

"He is brilliant," John said. "And his

66

mother had him tutored in advance of his years before she passed away. Penelope enjoyed directing his studies and worked with him until it was beyond her strength. Richard was devastated when his mother could no longer help him."

"How sad for him!"

"Sad for all of us," John said, with a sober glance her way. "This has not been a happy place. Richard's health has suffered as a result. Dr. Gideon hopes that with your advent my son's spirits may improve, and his physical well-being also."

"I trust that will be the case," she said. "I have been given to understand that this Dr. Gideon is rather aged and beyond his prime. Have you thought to call in some other physician to examine the boy?"

John Stone stopped in his tracks and stared at her angrily. "Who has been talking to you about Dr. Gideon? My brother?"

"I really don't know," she said in confusion. "I meant no offense. Nor any condemnation of the doctor. I was thinking only of your son."

He seemed to unbend a little. "My son is doing well under Dr. Gideon's care. I have a strong faith in the old gentleman, in spite of his suffering from the normal infirmities of age. While he lives and is able to follow his profession no other medical man will enter my door."

They resumed their short walk to the main entrance of the house. John Stone was surely touchy on the subject. Sarah wished that Rodney had warned her of this as well so she could have avoided an awkward moment. She couldn't help wondering why the master of Dankhurst was so firm in his faith in the old physician. Surely it could not be for the reason the villagers maintained?

They came to the fountain and its lily pond, and Sarah thought how much it would add to the beauty of the courtyard if it had been kept in repair. But the slimy green water of the pond and the stark dry center post were symbolic of the decay that was beginning to encompass all of the estate, the decay for which the mental state of the man at her side was responsible.

She paused by the circular pond and stared at their reflections in the stagnant water, with its litter of leaves and other debris. Their outlines were clearly defined in it, and she said, "The water seems very deep. Is it?"

He frowned at their mirrored figures. "Not really. It's only about a foot deep.

Penelope had a great interest in the fountain and pond. She considered it the outstanding decoration on the grounds. I shut the fountain off the night of her death. I have had no desire to see it in operation since."

With that he resumed the walk to the porch and front door. Sarah made no comment, but she felt that this could not be the action of a man who had been responsible for his wife's death. It had been as cruelly wrong of the villagers to accuse John Stone of poisoning Penelope as it had been of Amelia Gordon to viciously accuse Sarah of John Gordon's murder. Perhaps John Stone might be deemed at fault for his stubborn determination to use no other doctor but the infirm Dr. Gideon. Beyond that, she was sure he was blameless. And in this instance was he not merely showing loyalty to an old and respected family friend?

John broke into her reverie as he held open the heavy oaken door for her. "Now you shall see the living room," he promised.

Sarah followed him down the hallway and through the double doors. It was a magnificent room, with a bank of windows at one end decorated with wine drapes, and a graceful white fireplace at the other. It was furnished — almost cluttered — with a profusion of antique pieces, and a fine Persian rug covered a great area of the hardwood floor. The walls were papered in a pale rose with a floral pattern in a deeper shade. The ceiling curved gently upward from the walls, with complex patterns and scrolls in its plaster, and two huge crystal chandeliers gave the room an added air of elegance. Portraits in elaborate gold frames were hung about the room.

"What a lovely room!" was Sarah's reaction as she gazed about her.

John Stone nodded and led her directly to a portrait in dark tones above the fireplace. From the golden frame an old man slumped in a chair, which was likely still part of this room's furnishings, stared glumly at them, his withered hands caressing the arms of the chair.

"That's my maternal grandfather, Stephen Dank," John said. "He was the builder of the house. This painting was done just a year or so before his death when he was an old man."

"He has a strong face."

"He was a rugged individualist," John Stone said. "Perhaps he might even be termed an eccentric. Yet he made his mark and built this place well." He moved on to show her other portraits of the family.

At length they came to a place where a rectangle of a lighter shade on the wall revealed that it was a space in which a portrait had once hung and had recently been removed. She turned to him with a questioning smile. "Do we have one missing here?"

"My wife's," he said with a strange expression on his sensitive face, and then moved on abruptly to point out a study of an aunt long dead.

Sarah was disturbed that his wife's portrait had been taken down, and could only assume that his grief at her loss was so deep he could not bear to enter the room and see the beloved face. They looked at several other family paintings, and then she suddenly found herself standing before the last one yet to be considered. It was on the wall next to the double doors, and she hesitated before it, although John Stone tried to lead her on.

It was the portrait of a strikingly lovely dark-haired young woman in a low-cut red gown that highlighted her extravagant beauty. Only an expression of arrogance marred the smile of the painting's subject. But what startled Sarah was the shocking

71

tear that had been made in the canvas, almost diagonally across the portrait, so that the face was slashed and mutilated.

"Such a lovely painting! And so badly damaged!" Sarah said with a gasp of dismay as she turned to the tall blond man at her side. "Who is it, and what happened?"

The pallor of John's face was now invaded by a spot of crimson at each of his cheek bones. In a choked voice he said, "I did not mean to have you dwell on this one. It was damaged by vandals one night when most of the household were absent."

"How awful!" she said, staring at the painting again. "And who did you say this was?"

Before he could reply Abigail Durmot came in to join them. The soft-spoken young woman smiled and said, "I'm sorry to intrude, but lunch is ready and waiting."

"Of course," John Stone said with relief. "I had forgotten the time. You must be famished, Miss Bennett."

She smiled forlornly. "My appetite has hardly been of such dimensions. And we did eat heartily at the judge's last night."

John gave Abigail Durmot a smiling glance. "We must test our cook's abilities as compared with those of the judge's treasured Mrs. MacPherson."

The tour of the house was brought to an abrupt end. Not until later was Sarah to see the great ballroom with its glass-walled conservatory and profusion of plants, or the library and its hundreds of volumes, or John Stone's study and those dark, less accessible regions that were to play a prominent part in her sojourn at Dankhurst.

Rodney joined them for the excellent lunch of cold mutton, and kept Sarah entertained throughout the meal. It was on his shoulders that most of the conversation fell, for John said only an occasional word, and Abigail bent demurely over her plate without any comment. Sarah was puzzled by Penelope's attractive cousin and was beginning to wonder if her mask of quiet gentility covered a more spirited creature.

"But Edinburgh is the city of Mary, Queen of Scots," Rodney insisted over the tankard of ale, with which he was washing down the meal. "Holyrood Palace was her home for sixteen years. You must see her apartments, and Darnley's quarters as well. And the picture gallery, with portraits of over a hundred Scottish kings!"

"Were there that many?" Sarah asked in wonder.

John Stone made one of his few comments. "Hardly," he said. "The collection is remarkable chiefly for the artist's imagination!"

"Fantasy or no, it is a truly wondrous sight," Rodney insisted. "I intend to compose a ballad about Holyrood one day."

John gave his brother a sarcastic glance. "Do you, now? I have always felt you had more acquaintance and heart for the pubs of Edinburgh rather than the castles!"

Rodney took no offense but laughed and thumped the table with his fist. "I know my fair share of taverns and pubs too! And if Miss Bennett sees fit, I shall be pleased to take her on a tour of them."

"Thank you," she said with a polite smile. "I doubt if I have the constitution to properly enjoy the experience."

"No proper gentleman would offer you such an invitation," John Stone said, frowning at his brother. "Nor would he thump the table so as to disturb the china when he offered it."

Rodney touched his napkin to his lips, then tossed it by his plate as he rose to clap a hand on John's shoulder. "But, brother, I have no pretensions to gentility. No more than Bobbie Burns had!"

"Too bad you lack Burns' other talents," John said coldly.

Rodney remained good-humored. "But I do match him in at least one thing. I can drink a prodigious quantity of our native whisky!" And laughing, he sauntered out of the dining room.

There was a silence in the dark-paneled dining room after he left. And then John gave Sarah a resigned glance. "You must not take my brother's sense of humor as typical of Scotland," he said. "He is a strange person."

She smiled. "I find him amusing." And she glanced Abigail's way for the possibility of some support, but that pretty little mouse was again avoiding anyone's eyes with a concentrated study of the tablecloth.

"When you are ready I'll take you up to see my son," John said. "No doubt after that you will be repairing to your room for rest. You must be fatigued after your journey."

"I am a trifle tired," she admitted as she rose from the table. And to Abigail, she said with a smile, "I think your supervision of the kitchen must be excellent if this meal is a sample."

The quiet Abigail showed a wan smile of pleasure. "We do much better at dinner," she assured her in her small voice.

John escorted Sarah from the room, and as they passed the double doors to the living room she again had an impulse to query him more about the damaged portrait and who its subject was, but he kept up a continuous chatter, in contrast to his silence in the dining room. As a result, she had no opportunity to pose her questions.

"My son's bedroom is on your floor," John said in his sober way as they started up the stairs. "His is at the rear of the house."

"Do these spells of fever last long?"

"Not as a rule," he said. "Richard seems to be weakened by them, but he quickly regains his normal health after a few days."

"Has he always suffered from this condition?"

He sighed. "No. It first showed up after his mother's death. And since then he has had attacks at fairly regular intervals."

"I see," she said quietly.

She followed him down a dim silent hallway to a door at the very end. He opened the door and ushered her into a large bedroom in which the curtains had been drawn and the heavy odor of illness filled the air. Sarah had an impulse to pull back the curtains and open the windows, and let some sunshine and air into the stuffy room.

John Stone went over to a broad bed under whose coverings a small figure stirred. Sarah stared through the shadows and made out the wan features of a delicate little blond boy, whose long hair fell unkemptly across his forehead and about his ears. He was a small, frail edition of John Stone.

His father announced, "This is Miss Bennett, Miss Sarah Bennett. She has come to be your companion and teacher."

The white face on the pillow showed a smile. "Can you teach me Latin, Miss Bennett?"

She smiled back at him. "When you are feeling better I'm sure I can at least offer you an introduction to it."

"My mummy was going to begin me with Latin," Richard said plaintively, "but she didn't have time to get around to it."

"I'll look at my Latin books so I'll be ready," Sarah promised. "Just you get better soon."

"I will," the boy promised. "Can I go downstairs tomorrow, Father?"

"We'll see," John Stone said. "It all depends. If not, Miss Bennett will begin your studies up here."

The little boy's face brightened. "I'm glad you've come, Miss Bennett. I have hardly any friends except Rodney."

"I'm sure it must be lonely for you here with only grown-ups for company," Sarah said. And turning to his father, "Aren't there any of the neighbors' or your tenants' children to offer Richard companionship of his own age?"

John Stone showed no expression. "We haven't any near neighbors, and the tenants and their offspring are not friendly to us at Dankhurst."

"I had forgotten," she said hastily.

"You should provide plenty of companionship for him," the blond man said almost harshly. "I'll leave you two to get acquainted."

And to avoid your being asked any more embarrassing questions, Sarah thought. She said, "I'd enjoy remaining with Richard a little longer."

"Not more than a few minutes, please," John Stone warned her. "Dr. Gideon wants him to have plenty of quiet."

"Of course," she said. And then, "Doesn't the room strike you as warm and stuffy? Wouldn't a little fresh air be beneficial?"

John Stone shook his head. "Dr. Gideon wants the room to be in darkness and the windows closed so Richard will relax and get his rest. He feels that is the most important thing for him. And I must agree." He nodded, turned, and strode out of the room.

Sarah gazed after him with angry frustration, feeling that Dr. Gideon must be a dunce, and John Stone as well. Surely it was basic that a sick youngster required fresh air and sunshine.

Richard spoke up from the pillow in his piping voice. "Before Mummy died she taught me all my lessons."

"I know," Sarah said gently. "And I think that was wonderful."

"I miss her," the boy said.

"Of course. I can never hope to take her place with you, but I'll do my best to make your lessons interesting."

"Thank you," Richard said. "I'll tell her."

Sarah stared down at the wan, childish face, and a feeling of sheer horror crept over her. A chilling atmosphere suddenly filled the shadowed room. "Tell her?" she echoed.

"Yes," Richard said, raising himself on an elbow to confide in her. "Sometimes she comes to me at night. She stands at the foot of my bed. And even though I can't see her clearly, I know she's watching over me, and I talk to her."

4

Sarah tried hard to conceal the shock the youngster's words gave her. She said, "Of course we all have dreams in which our loved ones return. It is one of nature's means of healing our grief."

"But I'm awake when I see her," Richard insisted. "It is the creaking of the floor-boards when she comes in the room that wakes me from sleep."

"You must tell me more about it another time," Sarah said easily, for want of a better means of getting free of an awkward situation. "But now you must lie back and rest, as your father and Dr. Gideon want."

"Dr. Gideon is old and silly," the boy said fretfully. "I would like some fresh air, as you said."

She smiled. "I'm sure your father knows best. You settle down and rest awhile longer." She fixed the coverlet over him, and touched her hand gently to his soft yellow hair as he stared up at her from the pillow. "Perhaps we can go out together to-morrow."

"I like you," Richard said. And then, in a chilling addition: "My mummy will like you, too."

She forced herself to smile, then quickly withdrew from the room and closed the door after her. She stood for a full moment, terror on her pretty face as she stared into the shadows of the hallway and wondered what sort of household this might be.

The child had spoken of his mother's ghostly appearances in the most matter-of-fact manner. So much so, that she had found herself filled with a strange fear. Either the boy had a strikingly vivid imagination, or something was going on in this house that sorely required explanation.

Still shaken by her talk with the boy, she made her way to the front of the house and her own room. When she arrived there the door was partly open, though she was certain she had left it shut. And as she paused before the doorway she had the eerie knowledge that someone was in the room!

Nervously she took the knob in her hand and pushed the door full open to see Abigail Durmot standing before the dresser. Hearing her, the attractive young woman turned quickly, surprise showing in her face. Apparently the demure Abigail had been investigating Sarah's room and had not expected her to return so soon.

Sarah, standing just inside the door, said, "How nice of you to visit me. I'm sorry I wasn't here to welcome you."

The other girl was badly flustered, her cheeks flaming. "I tried the door and it swung open," she improvised quickly. "I came in thinking you might soon return."

"And so I have," Sarah said with a little smile. "Won't you sit down?"

"Thank you." Abigail took the nearest chair and sat hunched in it awkwardly.

Sarah stood facing her. "I am well pleased with my room," she said. "I'm certain I'm going to like it here."

"Yes," Abigail Durmot said in her small voice. "There is one thing I wanted to warn you about. I couldn't help overhearing your discussion of it with John."

"Oh?"

"The portrait in the living room," Abigail hurried on. "The one that has been slashed across its face. You mentioned it to John. You asked him who the subject of the portrait was."

"Yes," Sarah admitted, recalling the moment and John's reaction to it — his unwillingness to reveal the identity of the arrogantly lovely face.

Abigail gave her a frightened look. "That was the picture of his dead half sister, Justine. He does not want her ever spoken of in this house. I'm sure you've heard how unhappy he is about her tragic death."

"I have heard a version of the story," she agreed. "But as a stranger, I made the error quite unwittingly."

"I'm sure of that," Abigail's eyes fixed on her with so astute a glance that Sarah could no longer think of her as the demure little creature who moved about the great house like a shadow. She was certain there was another side to Abigail.

"So I cannot believe he will hold it against me," Sarah said.

"Certainly not," Abigail agreed. "I merely wanted to let you know."

"And that is a portrait of Justine!"

Abigail nodded. "She died in that fire in France long before I came to the house. Penelope confided in me that it was then that John became the solemn person he is now."

Sarah nodded. "He lacks the good humor of his brother."

The girl in the chair smiled. "Rodney is a one, isn't he? Yet I don't know what this old house would do without him. He gives it the little life it has. He and poor ailing Richard."

"I have seen the boy," Sarah said. "And it worries me the way his father follows out Dr. Gideon's rules in taking care of him. I fear the old man may be wrong in his prescriptions."

"Penelope worried about the boy before her death," Abigail said with a troubled expression. "As she grew weaker she had strange fancies. And she begged me to stay on in the house to protect the boy."

She frowned. "You say your cousin had strange fancies? What sort of fancies?"

"The sort better not spoken of," Abigail said.

"You have roused my curiosity; surely you will satisfy it?"

Abigail looked about her uneasily, and then leaning forward in the chair, said, "If I tell you, you must promise not to say a word to John."

"Very well."

Abigail hesitated and then, her eyes wide with fear, she began to talk in a low voice. "When I came here Penelope was already well advanced in the illness that took her, although she lived on for almost a full year. But she confided in me that she and John had lately had several bitter quarrels. She had accused him of having been in love with his half sister and allowing her death to sour him. For it was well known to all that Justine was mad about John and left Dankhurst in a wild anger because John had made Penelope his wife. She never returned alive."

"I have heard the story," Sarah said.

"Penelope could not stand John's continual moping and his delving into ancient secrets in the library. Especially she did not like his dwelling on poisons and poisoners. And when he began to spend long periods of time investigating the circumstances of Priscilla Kirk's history and suicide she voiced her objections in the strongest manner."

Sarah nodded. "Priscilla Kirk was his ancestor, who was wrongly accused of poisoning someone and took her own life."

"Yes," Abigail said. "And her spirit has since been said to haunt this house. It was Penelope's contention that John had transferred his fixation from Justine to the wraith of Priscilla Kirk. And in a way had come under the romantic spell of a ghostly creature."

"In one sense that could have been true," Sarah said.

"My dying cousin was obsessed with the idea," Abigail said, her face and her tone revealing her fright. "And in her last weeks she began to murmur wildly about visitations at night! Of the legendary Priscilla Kirk coming to her room and mocking her! In truth, I was sure Penelope had fallen into a kind of madness. And it was then that she prayed I would not desert Richard. She feared that when she was gone the ghost of Priscilla would prey on the child. I tried to reassure her, but it was no use. She died believing her little boy was in danger from a wraith who had claimed her husband for her own."

Sarah heard out Abigail's story with all the ominous feelings she had known in the shadowed room of the child a little earlier. The two stories seemed to connect. Richard had been so certain that a specter had made visits to his bedside, a specter he took to be his mother, but whom he had not seen clearly enough to identify. And now she was hearing how Penelope herself had been harassed by similar visitations. And how she had been convinced that the spirit she had seen was none other than that of the long-dead Priscilla Kirk. It had been Penelope's fear that on her death the jealous wraith would turn to her son to torment. Surely, if Richard was not giving rein to his childish imagination, this is what must have happened.

Taking a deep breath, she asked Abigail, "Do you believe in ghosts?"

Abigail hesitated for a moment. "Yes."

"What evidence makes you say that?"

"It was a ghost who slashed Justine's portrait! The jealous ghost of Priscilla Kirk! That's what all the servants say."

Sarah frowned. "John Stone told me it was done by vandals."

"So he says. But what vandals? How could they get in here with servants in the house all the time? He knows who did it, but he doesn't want to admit it."

"You honestly believe that?"

"I do." The girl leaned forward again. "And that is why he took down Penelope's portrait. He took it down and hid it away somewhere, because he knew if he left it there, her vengeful spirit would come in the night and slash it as well!"

"But that is a fantastic story!"

Abigail's eyes gleamed triumphantly. She was no longer the mouselike young girl she'd seemed earlier. "Then why did he take the portrait down?" she asked.

It was a perplexing question. "I'm new here; I can't imagine."

"And why has he brought you here?" Abigail went on.

Sarah was startled. "To care for his son, of course."

Abigail shook her head slowly as she got to her feet. "No," she told Sarah. "It was she who made him bring you here!"

"She?"

"The ghost! She has bewitched him so that all he thinks about is poisons and the like. That is what sent him to follow your trial in Edinburgh, and why he felt so sorry for you."

Sarah was shocked. "You don't actually think that?"

"I do," Abigail insisted. "But there is danger in it for you. Now that you are here she will be jealous as long as you remain under this roof. She will be wanting to get rid of you in the same way she worked her hateful spells on Penelope until she died."

"You're suggesting that Penelope was killed by a spirit's influence?"

"I am," Abigail said defiantly. "Dr. Gideon could not diagnose her illness. And the villagers blamed John for poisoning her. But I know better. I know it was something from beyond that kept grinding at her. It was Priscilla Kirk who caused her death!"

"You mustn't say such things!" Sarah protested. "Especially not where the boy can hear you. No wonder he has all kinds of daft notions!"

"Indeed, and has he?" Abigail asked softly as she stared into Sarah's face.

Sarah was on her guard at once. "I thank you for telling me all you have, although I must confess I do not go along with your theories. I find it impossible to share your belief in the avenging ghosts of long-dead beauties. No doubt you are right in saying that John Stone has become too morbidly interested in the past. I can surely agree with you there."

"I am glad you have come," Abigail Durmot said. "I do not know how long I care to remain here. And I would not want to leave with young Richard having no protector."

Sarah gave her a questioning smile. "But are you not interested in Rodney Stone?"

It was Abigail's turn to smile demurely. "It is true I like him. And I have reason to believe that he is fond of me. But nothing will come of it; Rodney is not the marrying kind. He is too jealous of his freedom and the bottle!"

"He may change."

"Not ever! Not Rodney!"

"And there is no romantic attachment between yourself and John Stone?"

Abigail shook her head. "He has never had eyes for me. I will not deny he is a handsome man, but I have never been interested in him. The villagers with their spiteful tongues had it that he murdered Penelope for the love of me!" She gave a bitter laugh. "It shows how much they really know about what goes on within these walls."

Sarah shrugged. "I have had an unhappy history myself. I hope my coming here has not been another dreadful mistake. I have a friend, the judge who presided at my trial in Edinburgh, who has asked me to keep in touch with him and who is willing to see to my getting a fresh start somewhere else if need be."

"It will depend on her," Abigail said. "Wait! You will find out soon enough without need of a warning from me." She moved to the door. "I must go down to the kitchen and see that dinner is properly under way."

Sarah slumped down into a chair as soon as she had gone. Abigail's weird story had served to increase her fears. She had come to the room in a nervous state because of Richard's strange talk, only to have an even odder picture of affairs in the old mansion given her. She was not certain about Abigail.

Had the pretty brown-haired girl been trying to frighten her? If so, she had succeeded very well! Or had she told a ghostly tale in which she honestly believed? Sarah couldn't accept this. Abigail had presented such a different side to her just now that she was more than ever convinced that the quiet modest exterior was a pose to disguise her true personality.

The protests that she was not interested in John Stone also lacked sincerity. And Sarah found herself wondering if Abigail were not guilty of some diabolical scheme to snare the handsome master of Dankhurst for herself. How convenient for Abigail to spread this story of the avenging wraith of Priscilla Kirk as a cloak for her own evil actions.

Abigail could have administered some poison to her cousin until she finally died. Abigail could have slashed the portrait of the dead Justine simply because she had once claimed John's affection and to help make her story of the ghost ring true! And it could be Abigail who was entering the child's room and standing in the shadows pretending to be the ghost of his mother. It would be easy for Abigail to be guilty in every instance!

Sarah knew she must keep this carefully in mind, for if the supposedly demure Abigail turned out to be the dangerous enemy she faced here, she must take certain precautions. The incessant talk of ghosts, poison, and murders made her head reel. She had come to Rawlwyn thinking to leave all this behind her, only to find herself plunged once again into the mysterious complexities of a household gripped by a hidden terror.

How few of these secret fears were ever known to the outside world! Yet it seemed as if almost every great house and every single family unit had its dark shadow that must be hidden. Or perhaps a horrifying vice or weakness that must be concealed behind closed shutters. So it went. And once again Sarah found herself a helpless pawn in a house of strangers. A party to some sort of evil of which she had not even a scant knowledge. She had a compulsion to write the judge at once and ask that she might return to Edinburgh. And then she realized she was being childish. She had only just arrived. She must at least give the post a short trial. And one fact stood out in her mind: Richard Stone was badly in need of a friend.

Dinner was served by the light of flickering candles set out in tall silver candlesticks. Again Rodney was the life of the party while the others listened silently or made only occasional remarks. And once more the food was excellent.

With dinner over, Abigail Durmot and John Stone entered into a serious discussion about some household matter and the two went off down the hall to his study. It remained for Rodney to accompany Sarah to the living room, where one of the great crystal chandeliers had been lighted to provide a subdued glow that filled the big room.

Rodney looked the dandy in a dark blue coat with shiny brass buttons, and a string black tie at his wing collar. He waved at the portraits along the walls, "You have seen our vaunted picture gallery?"

"Yes," she said. "I found them most interesting."

He smiled. "A parcel of rogues and ladies of easy virtue!"

"Come now," she reproved him as she sat in an easy chair, "that is no fit way to discuss your ancestors."

"There were exceptions," Rodney was willing to admit. "But they are not my favorites of the lot."

She laughed. "You delight in shocking people, don't you?"

"Not at all. I merely believe in being frank."

"Doesn't that often amount to the same thing?"

"In truth it does," Rodney agreed. "And are you still not aware that you have jumped from the frying pan into the fire?"

"Are you asking me if I'm happy here? Yes, I still think I may enjoy these surroundings." She was not about to let him know her private doubts and fears at this point.

He folded his arms and studied her with interest. "You are such a bonny wee lass. And yet you are not fairly equipped with good sense."

"Why do you say that?"

"If you had any brains you'd pick up your skirts and show this old fortress your heels!"

She smiled. "Is that the advice you give every new governess?"

"When I like them as much as I do you," he said. "Only it happens you are our first."

"Then I'm somewhat of a novelty in the house," she said.

"A disturbing novelty where my heart is

concerned," Rodney assured her, coming to stand near her. "It would be easy to fall in love with a girl like you."

"So well rehearsed!" she teased. "I know you have said it often."

He laughed. "Not more than a score of times. I swear it!"

"The story goes you have left a trail of broken hearts from here to Edinburgh and Glasgow and back," Sarah said. "I have been warned about you."

"Now that angers me!" Rodney said without losing his amused expression. "They have poisoned your mind against me, if you will pardon the allusion."

She colored. "You need not apologize."

"I'm sorry," he said contritely. "It was an unintentional slip. I have no wish to make you unhappy by bringing up an unpleasant shadow from your past."

"I am certain of that," she said. "So let us dwell no more on it."

"Agreed!" He smiled and reached out to take her hand in his and hold it. "I only ask that you keep open views about me until I have proved my sincerity where you are concerned."

"I'm no match for your wiles," she protested.

"When I no longer have an eye for a

pretty girl then I shall be under six feet of our good Scottish earth. To flirt is to live. But into every man's life there must come at least one serious love. Who can tell but that you are mine?"

"What a pretty speech," she said with admiration. "I do not mind hearing it as long as you don't expect me to take you seriously."

"You are here to be governess to young Richard," he told her. "Your position will require that you reprimand him from time to time — not his uncle!"

"But his uncle so requires it," she teased.

With a show of despair the dandified Rodney dropped her hand and turned away to regard the portrait of Justine on the wall near him. "By all that's mighty," he exclaimed, "I must say you are as flawed as that fair lass."

"You are referring to Justine?"

He turned to her. "I was, and to you. So you know whose portrait that is."

"Yes. And I wonder who was so cruel as to mutilate it."

Rodney again glanced at the marred lovely face with the great slash across it. "The story is that vandals did it."

"That is the story. But what do you believe?"

He looked at her with a mocking gleam in his eyes. "But I am an innocent. How should I know?"

"Of course you're not indulging in your usual frankness now," she said. "Is it that you fear to tell the truth?"

"I prefer to accept the theory of vandals," Rodney said lightly. "But you must admit my sister was a true beauty."

"She was indeed."

He sighed. "I have heard from John that she was so burned by the fire that destroyed her cottage that what was left of her face was not recognizable. So exits beauty!"

Sarah was about to make a reply when her glance went past him to the hallway and she gave a tiny gasp. For materializing from the shadows was a face as wrinkled and ugly as any she had seen. A tall, weird-looking old woman, dressed completely in black, advanced from the hallway to stand before them, her hands folded primly.

Rodney turned to her and said, "Good evening, Mrs. Fergus."

"Good evening," the woman replied in a cold voice. Her gray hair was drawn tightly back from her face. "I am looking for Mr. John," she said.

"My brother is in his study with Miss

Abigail," Rodney said pleasantly. "I'm sure he won't mind your going down there." And turning to Sarah, he said, "This is Mrs. Fergus, who served as companion and housekeeper for Penelope until Abigail came to take the position. Mrs. Fergus is now in charge of the kitchen and the domestic staff."

Sarah smiled at the elderly woman. "I'm happy to meet you, Mrs. Fergus. I am Sarah Bennett, governess to Richard."

Mrs. Fergus gave a sniff. "When his mother was alive she was all the governess he needed!"

"But his mother is no longer alive," Sarah said gently. "So someone must take on the task."

"I am well aware of that," the older woman said. "Things have come to a sorry pass since Miss Penelope's death."

"You must be willing to accept change." Rodney smiled at her.

"Not when it concerns the poor dear bairn I raised from the cradle," the tall, gaunt-faced woman said in her cold fashion. "If you will excuse me, I will go now to Mr. John."

She vanished into the shadows with a rustle of her black skirts, and Rodney turned to Sarah with a grimace and a shrug. "You see we have lunatics of every variety here. Mrs. Fergus was Penelope's nurse and companion. Her devotion to her was tinged with madness. Now she hates us all because Penelope is dead. She will not even show kindness to poor little Richard."

"She is indeed a strange woman."

"One I advise you not to cross," Rodney warned.

She smiled in surprise. "Gracious! You actually make her sound sinister!"

"Her mind is tainted," Rodney said frankly. "I do not trust such people, nor do I like them around me. It is mistaken kindness on my brother's part to allow her to remain at Dankhurst."

Changing the subject, Sarah said, "When I talked with Richard he was at pains to inform me you were his friend."

Rodney's handsome, devil-may-care countenance took on a pleased smile. "The boy does like me."

"I am sure of it."

His smile vanished. "If Richard were my son I'd whisk him away from this place in a twinkling. I would not let him stay here another night."

"Why do you feel so strongly about this?"

"The boy is being treated like a delicate

flower and encouraged to waste away. That dotard Dr. Gideon can do nothing for him. He should have the best medical attention in Edinburgh, and his father refuses to give it to him."

"What is this I refuse to give my son?" John Stone demanded, entering the room, his face showing anger.

"The attentions of a proper doctor — or doctors — in Edinburgh," Rodney said defiantly.

"Richard is my son," John said flatly. "I will do what I consider best for him."

"We've heard that tune before," Rodney said. He bowed to Sarah. "It is not possible for me to remain here longer; I cannot promise control of my temper. Good night, Miss Bennett." And with an angry glance at John, he left to go out by the front door.

John turned to her. "I'm glad I took the opportunity of warning you against him earlier."

"He is not that bad," she said.

John's eyebrows raised. "I'm shocked to hear you say that, Miss Bennett."

"It is apparent there is a bitter enmity between you two," she said.

"I won't deny that," John said. Then, "There is a moon and the night is mild. Would you care to stroll in the courtyard a little before retiring?"

Sarah got up with a smile. "It does sound inviting."

The silver moonlight shone on the statues dotted over the lawns causing them to stand out like ghostly sentinels. It was an awe-inspiring sight. She clung to John Stone's arm as they strolled quietly along the gravel path. In the distance crickets chirped, and at intervals came the harsh cry of a night bird.

John Stone spoke in the darkness. "Let me tell you, Miss Bennett, your arrival at Dankhurst has given me a new peace of mind."

"Thank you," she said.

"In spite of what Rodney or the others believe, I am deeply concerned with my son's welfare," he went on. "It was his mother's wish that Dr. Gideon continue to attend him. As long as the doctor is well enough I will not make a change."

"Your decision is based on a sentimental reason then," she pointed out.

"So be it," he said stubbornly. "I'm deeply engaged in a new phase of my research at this time and I do not have patience for the boy. In any event, every sight of him re-minds me of his mother and my loss."

"His loss also, and no fault of the boy's."

"Agreed," John Stone said in an unhappy voice. "From the moment I first saw you in the courtroom I could tell you were a person of high moral values and great heart. And I determined that you should be the one to take the place of Richard's mother, so far as the boy is concerned. I have talked to him tonight, and he tells me he has taken a great fancy to you. So I know I have done the right thing."

Sarah said, "I will do my best. But you must allow my view to prevail occasionally in his care."

John came to a halt by the pond. She could see the frown on his handsome face in the moonlight as he said, "We shall consider that in the future."

She sighed and gazed into the stagnant water of the pond, made a mirror now by the moonlight and given an eerie beauty it did not possess by daylight. She could see her own reflection and John's in startling detail. And as she stared into the water a third reflection suddenly appeared there with them — a face so horrible of countenance and wearing such an expression of sheer hatred that she could not help crying out.

John looked at her in alarm. "What is wrong?"

She pointed to the pond. "In there! Just now! I saw the most awful face!"

He frowned and looked in the water. "I see only our own reflections!"

Sarah glanced there again and admitted, "It's gone. But I know I saw it!" She turned and looked up at the windows above them. "It was as if someone were peering out of one of those windows at us."

"I think your nerves are playing tricks on you," John Stone said calmly. "You are tired. You should go to bed at once."

5

John Stone saw Sarah to the door of her room, and she noted that someone had lighted a lamp with an ornate porcelain bowl and plain glass chimney and placed it on her dresser. It provided the room with a meager illumination, but she supposed she could manage with it. The master of Dankhurst seemed to be still upset by her insistence that she'd seen the hate-distorted face.

He paused at her door. "You are sure you feel all right? Would you care for a glass of sherry? Or perhaps some hot cocoa?"

"No, please don't concern yourself," she begged.

"Your vision below has worried me," he readily admitted.

"Perhaps you were right," she said. "It could have been a trick played by the moonlight and a tired mind." She knew this was not so, but decided it was better not to make any more of it.

He seemed relieved by her words. "So much has happened in the past twenty-four hours. Do try to get a good rest." He bowed, and she went inside and closed the door after bidding him good night.

She lost no time preparing for bed. When she had donned her nightgown and combed out the black hair, which reached to well below her waist, she was utterly tired.

The old mansion was strangely silent. She stood by the lamp, reluctant to lower the wick and blow out the tiny flame that stood between her and darkness. In spite of her brave show for John Stone, the stories she'd heard during the day and the memory of that dreadful face in the pond still lingered in her mind. She left the lamp and moved to the window, a graceful figure in her full-skirted nightgown and flowing dark tresses.

At the window she parted the heavy drapes to stare down at the courtyard and the pond, now a circle of silver in the moonlight. Her gaze shifted to the lawns and the statues that stood about on the grounds. The figures of long-dead gentry set out there by Stephen Dank because of who knew what strange whim! No wonder the servants believed the estate haunted and poachers shied away from it as though a plague lingered there.

In a very real way a plague of sorts had taken hold of the gray-stone mansion — a plague of fear! And she was now also caught up in this spider's web of strange events and terror. Yet a day ago she had escaped from the shadow of a death sentence, so why should she let a few weird tales and this old house frighten her? It was too absurd! And bolstering herself with that thought, she closed the drapes, and while the boldness of her new mood persevered she forced herself to put out the lamp and plunge the room into velvety blackness.

A moment later she was in bed and pulling the cool, somewhat damp sheets, over her. Her head touched the pillow, her eyelids closed, and she sank into a deep sleep.

It was a dreamless slumber that couldn't have lasted long. She came awake gradually, vexed to see that it was still pitch dark and annoyed at this interruption of her rest, without fully realizing what had awakened her.

In a moment she found out: She heard shuffling footsteps just above her, hurried footsteps; then a door slammed from somewhere over her head! She frowned. But that was the fourth floor, the floor that John had explicitly told her was not in use. A deserted area of the house!

Now there was a loud cry, as of someone in pain, a cry so eerie that it caused a chill to run along Sarah's spine! She sat up, her eyes wide with alarm. She was fully awake and alert to any sound from above. Then she heard a kind of moaning or sobbing that lasted for only a few seconds; another door slammed, and then silence!

Sarah remained sitting up in bed, staring into the darkness. Sleep had vanished; she was now wide awake. She remembered seeing a short candle in a clay holder on her bedside table, with a tiny box of matches beside it. Groping blindly in the darkness, she located the matches and struck a light. By its small flame she found the candle and touched the match to its wick. At least the gloom was pierced by a token glow from the candle, although she could see little by its light.

She was still sitting up in bed when she heard the footsteps coming softly down the hall toward her door. She swung out of bed, put on her dressing gown, and stood staring at the door, her pretty face showing fear. She remained there, motionless, watching the door, listening . . . waiting. . . .

It was almost as if she'd expected the soft knock on the door. And then her name was called out in an urgent whisper, and the gentle knocking was repeated. Like a person in a trance, she moved slowly across the room and placed her ear against one of the door's wooden panels.

"Sarah! Sarah Bennett!" The whisper came urgently again.

"What do you want?" she asked nervously.

"Sarah!" Again the hoarse whisper.

"Who is it?" she asked, her hand on the bolt to slide it open.

"Please, don't keep me waiting out here!" the whisper came clearly.

After seconds of indecision Sarah slid the bolt and opened the door a fraction. She could see no one in the darkness of the hallway. Her caution partially deserting her, she opened the door farther and stared out. Still no one. Had it been some sort of hoax? Perhaps a bad joke on Rodney's part? He could be a devil!

Sarah took a step into the dark hallway, leaving the door wide open for a fast retreat. And then it struck! Someone she could not see, but whose harsh breathing she could hear! Strong hands grappled with her, and she felt a swishing movement come close to her and was conscious of her clothes ripping at the same time. She fought back her attacker and screamed out her fear as loud as she could, crying for help.

Her attacker made a weird sobbing sound, and bony fingers of great strength grasped Sarah's throat in an effort to shut off her screams. Sarah fought for her life. For a brief moment she freed her throat of that terrible pressure and in a strangled voice cried for help once again.

This time she heard John Stone shout from the other side of the house, "What's wrong? . . . Who's screaming?"

The sound of John's voice sent her attacker scurrying off into the darkness. Sarah gave a small moan of relief and staggered toward her own door. She closed it behind her, and leaning there weakly, slid the bolt in place.

Now John Stone was outside her door. "Miss Bennett, was that you? What is it?"

Before she could reply she saw to her complete consternation that her attacker had slit and slashed both her dressing gown and her nightgown to ribbons across the front. She could not present herself to John in this condition!

Folding the shreds of her gown about her, she spoke to him through the door. "I had a nightmare. I woke up screaming. I'm all right now."

"Are you certain?" He sounded unconvinced.

She touched a hand to her aching throat, knowing the dreadful risk she was taking in keeping the attack secret from him. "Please don't worry about me. I'm sure I'll be able to sleep again."

There was no reply for a moment as he apparently stood there, waiting. "Very well," he said reluctantly. "If you feel nervous again, don't hesitate to call for me."

"I promise," she said.

She heard his retreating footsteps, and then there was nothing but silence. She would have been almost ready to believe her own story of a nightmare, except for her aching throat and tattered clothes.

She was trembling, and her thoughts were chaotic. Why, she wondered dully, had she not found something to cover her and opened the door to confess the truth to John Stone? As it was, he would think her a foolish girl afraid of the darkness. In her panic she had probably done the wrong thing, but too late to worry about that now.

Checking the door to make sure it was

safely bolted, she went to get the candle and took it with her to the washstand, where she poured some cold water into the basin and bathed her aching neck. She next took off her torn clothes and found another nightgown to put on. At last she was back in bed, with the sheets pulled over her and the flickering candle still burning. She was far too frightened to put it out and decided she would let it burn out. Now she tried to form some picture of the creature who had made the wild attack on her. So dark had the hallway been, so quickly had everything happened, that she was at a loss to know who or what it might have been. Certainly ghosts didn't wield knives and tear one's clothes to bits!

Or did they? She recalled Abigail's insistence that it had been the ghost of Priscilla Kirk who had attacked Justine's portrait. Had she also been visited by the phantom figure of the long-dead girl? It was too absurd! And yet the attack had to be explained. She could not look to John for help after putting him off with a lie just now. She had let her embarrassment overcome her fear, and now she was faced with a new dilemma.

Of course there were her torn clothes. But if she were truly a hysterical female, she might rip them in that manner herself to bolster the story of her terrifying experience. Obviously she had placed herself in the position of having to keep the details of the attack secret. She would try to repair her torn things and be extremely careful in future not to foolishly expose herself to attack, as she had just done by going out into the hallway.

The bright sunshine filtering into her room around the heavy drapes let her know it was morning. The balance of her night after the mysterious attack had been uneventful. In fact, it would all seem like a dreadful nightmare now had it not been for her torn nightgown and robe on the nearby chair to remind her of the reality of her shattering experience.

She got up quickly and washed and dressed for breakfast. Downstairs she found only Rodney at the big table in the dining room; he was wearing casual clothes, with his shirt open at the throat. He rose quickly, pulled out a chair for her next to him, and bid her good morning.

He looked at her with a twinkle in his black eyes. "A night's rest has served you well," he said. "You are even prettier than I thought."

Sarah blushed as the maid entered to begin serving her breakfast. When the girl had left the room Sarah said, "I hope to begin my work with young Richard today."

Rodney looked interested. "I hope that you do. I understand the doctor is coming to visit him this morning. But that shouldn't take long." And with a bitter expression. "Or do much good, for that matter!"

"You do not seem to be an admirer of Dr. Gideon's."

"Judge him for yourself when you meet him," Rodney advised. And then, "I fancied I heard a great caterwauling in the middle of the night."

Sarah concentrated on her cereal. "Really?" she asked.

"I thought it might have disturbed you," he said, "since it seemed to be coming from your section of the house."

"I don't think I was aware of it."

He lifted his eyebrows. "Such a screaming! It hardly seems possible. And I thought I heard John's voice as well."

She looked up at him. "Are you certain it wasn't some nightmare of your own?"

He looked amused. "I am not given to nightmares," he said.

"A pity! I am told they are healthy. They

help preserve a sound mental state."

"Then whoever I heard last night must be possessed of a capital brain," the young man observed dryly.

Sarah was certain he was baiting her, that he knew more than he was letting on, but she could not imagine where he fitted into what had happened to her last night. Had he been her unknown assailant? It was possible, but she doubted it. Did he have an inkling of who it was? That seemed more likely. Was he protecting this person, or perhaps waiting in the shadows to be sure of his identity before denouncing him? She preferred this latter theory.

To change the subject she asked, "Since you know both cities so well, are you an Edinburgh or a Glasgow man?"

Rodney laughed, and putting on a thick brogue, said, "When Ah get drunk ona Setterday night, Glasca belongs tae me!"

It was her turn to smile. "You do the dialect very well," she said. "Yet you speak like an Englishman rather than a Scotsman.

"We pride ourselves on that at Dankhurst."

"So Glasgow is your favorite city?"

"Glasgow is a warm brawling place that can take you to its heart," Rodney said.

"And if you do not fall victim to her, you become a poet or a drunkard — or both, like me!"

"I see. And Edinburgh is another matter."

"Edinburgh is cold and reserved," he said, "filled with past glory. It's a paradise for the historian and not much for us, living in these stuffy times. Glasgow has a glamour, if only of a dirty variety, and all Edinburgh offers a Scotsman is sentimental excess, history in stone and dullness."

She had launched him on a subject of his liking, and he filled the balance of the breakfast period with his views on the two chief cities of Scotland. He escorted her out to the hallway and into the warm sunshine of the front porch, where he took his leave.

"It is my custom at this time of day to ride through the surrounding countryside for an hour or so," he said. "Are you fond of horses?"

"I like them," she said. "But I was brought up in the city and had no opportunity to ride them."

"Nothing equals the freedom of it on a morning like this," Rodney assured her. "Perhaps you could prevail on Abigail for the loan of a habit and the use of her sidesaddle. I'd be glad to give you some instruction."

She smiled. "I'll keep your offer in mind. But you mustn't forget that I am presently here in the role of an employee."

"I can't see John complaining because you take a notion to enjoy yourself," he said. Then glancing down the road that wound up to the mansion, he said, "If I'm not mistaken here comes Dr. Gideon's carriage now."

She looked down the road and saw the ancient black rig drawn slowly by a gray horse with scrawny shanks. "I'm glad he's arriving early," she said. "Then I'll be free to take charge of the boy."

"Perhaps," Rodney said; and with a nod to her, "I'll be going. I'm not up to a session with the learned doctor!" And he hurried from the veranda to vanish along the walk that led to the rear of the mansion and the stables.

Now the carriage was close, and she could see that a young, pock-marked boy, wearing an ill-fitting suit, a ridiculous little cap atop his thatch of unruly blond hair, was driving the rig. Beside him, slouched in an attitude of sleep, was a stout old man in rusty black and wearing a black stovepipe. His face was all folds, jowls, and

116

blotches. The carriage came to a halt, and the youth descended with great dignity.

As the youth gently shook him the old doctor came awake with a great snort and looked around him with glazed eyes. Seemingly aware of his arrival at Dankhurst, he bent forward to retrieve a small battered bag while the driver assisted him out of the carriage.

Dr. Gideon reached the gravel on legs that buckled for a fraction of a second, then pulled himself erect and came toward the veranda while the youth watched with bored eyes. Puffing, the doctor mounted the several steps, and the parchment folds of his droopy face gathered themselves into the semblance of a genial smile. "Ah, good day to you, Madam," he said, coming up to Sarah. "And how are you feeling today, Mrs. Stone?"

She stared at him in astonishment. "But I am not Mrs. Stone," she protested.

The doctor had removed his hat to reveal a shining bald head with a few random strands of white hair; his blotched face showed a smile of vexed amusement. "But of course you are not Mrs. Stone," he agreed in his wheezy voice. "That excellent lady passed away! A most melancholy event, and did I not treat her all through her lingering sickness? How could I have forgotten?" He paused to beam at her. "You are the cousin, of course — Miss Abigail!"

Sarah was distressed. "I am not Miss Abigail either."

"No?" The old man gave her an owlish stare. "But this is Dankhurst, is it not?" He glared over his shoulder at the youth standing by the carriage. "Or has that dunce brought me to the wrong place again?"

"No. You are in the right place," she assured him. "But I am new here. I have come to look after Richard and tutor him."

"Excellent!" The old man was smiling again and nodding his approval. "The boy is my patient. I must look at him at once."

She led the tottering old doctor into the hallway, astounded at his feeble condition and vague state of mind. No wonder the villagers regarded him as past his prime and Rodney had no patience with him. She could not imagine John Stone entrusting this ancient with the care of his wife and now allowing him to look after his ailing son. She was relieved to see John come striding down the hallway from his library to greet the old man.

"I'm glad you're here, Doctor," he said, shaking the veteran's emaciated hand. "I see you have already met Miss Bennett."

"Miss Bennett?" Dr. Gideon murmured absently, and then suddenly glanced her way with one of his forlorn smiles. "Oh, yes — Miss Bennett! Quite!"

"The boy is in his room waiting for you, Doctor. I think he is much better."

"Then I shall go directly up to him," Dr. Gideon announced, and made his way toward the stairs.

Sarah watched with a worried expression as he dragged himself up the stairs, clutching the railing for support. It was evident it was a task he would soon be unequal to. And then she looked at John Stone, standing beside her with his usual sober expression. She said, "Aren't you going up with him?"

He shook his head. "He prefers to examine the boy on his own."

"I see," she said. She was increasingly shocked that John should so rely on this man who was clearly in no proper state to carry on his practice. How could he be so blind? . . . unless the suspicions of the villagers were correct that he had an evil purpose and was using the old man to cover up his own black deeds!

He spoke through her reverie. "I gather by your expression that you are not im-

119

pressed by the good doctor."

"He is so very old and seems ill himself," she said.

"I agree he is but the shell of the man he once was."

"Knowing this, wouldn't you be wise to call in a second physician to diagnose the cause of your son's illness?"

The stubborn look, with which she was becoming so familiar, crossed John Stone's handsome face. "I think I explained that Penelope set great store by him, and it was her wish that he should attend the boy."

"But your wife herself was not helped by Dr. Gideon's ministrations," she ventured boldly.

"Are you accusing him of incompetence and suggesting that I am abetting him? If so, I have heard it before from the more ignorant of the villagers."

She felt her cheeks burn. "I only hoped to help."

"You can best do that by looking after the boy and having faith in Dr. Gideon. I assure you he was once the peer of any doctor in the county."

She said nothing more as they waited for the old man to return from his visit with the boy. It was plain that John was determined to keep the veteran physician on as his son's doctor. It only angered him to have his choice questioned.

Dr. Gideon finally appeared, making his way cautiously down the broad stairway, like an ancient crab. When he reached the bottom he smacked his purple lips and gave a deep sigh. Then, addressing himself to John Stone, he said, "The boy is much better. Really remarkable. I believe the powders I left for him have done their work well. There's no need to worry."

"That is good news, Doctor," John said gratefully. "And may Miss Bennett begin his studies now?"

The old man blinked and stared about him blankly as he said, "Miss Bennett?"

"This young woman who has come to instruct my son," John said, nodding toward her. "You met her earlier on the porch."

"Ah, yes." Dr. Gideon turned shakily to beam on her. "The attractive cousin. Why, yes, I think you may begin to work with the boy."

"I would like to take him outside for his lessons on pleasant days such as this," Sarah suggested. "Do you approve?"

"In moderation," the old man said solemnly. "His feeble constitution demands that his lungs be sheltered from too much harsh air. He should spend much of his time in a shaded room with the windows closed tight."

"But surely the stale air would be more injurious to him?"

The old man looked shocked that she should question his pronouncement. "I have dealt with these bleeding-from-the-lung conditions for half a century, Madam," he said with dignity. "Believe me when I say that a closed room is best for your son, except on the most balmy days." And with a nod, he moved toward the door.

His mention of Richard as her son had induced in her such a despair of his mental state that she gave John a long look and made no reply to the old doctor. John left to see Dr. Gideon on his way. After a few moments he returned, leaving the front door open. She could hear the creaking of the carriage wheels as the doctor was driven off.

John spoke before she could make mention of the old man's error, saying, "I know he called Richard your son. But that was only a slip of the tongue. When it comes to medical matters, I am sure he is as alert as ever. The proof is that Richard is much improved."

"Perhaps he would have improved in any

case," she said firmly. "May I take him down to the garden for his lessons?"

John hesitated. Then he said, "Providing you do not keep him in the sunshine too long. His constitution is frail and will not bear it, as the doctor told you."

She went upstairs in an angry mood. She could understand the old doctor's stupidity brought on by his age and illness but she couldn't reconcile herself to John's blind faith in the man. The door to Richard's room was partly ajar, and the boy was up and dressed, with Abigail standing beside him.

The little blond boy came running up to her with a delighted smile. "The doctor says that I am better. So I can go downstairs now and begin my studies with you." He linked one of his small hands in hers.

Abigail smiled. "I came up to see that he was dressed and ready for you."

"Thank you," Sarah said.

"Did you have a restful night?" Abigail asked in her quiet way.

Sarah thought it an odd question for this moment, then realized she was too sensitive because of what had happened, and replied pleasantly, "I managed well enough after I settled down."

"It takes time to adjust to a strange room

and bed," Abigail said.

"Yes," Sarah agreed. And then to the boy, "I plan to study in the garden. Is that agreeable to you?"

"I'd like that!" Richard said happily. "Can we go down now?"

"I see no reason why not." Sarah smiled at him, and with a nod to Abigail, she led him to the door and down the stairs. She wondered why the quiet cousin was showing so much interest in the boy. It was a new turn of events, by all accounts.

The decision to tutor Richard in the garden proved a happy one. He was delighted to be allowed to stay outdoors, and his mind proved even more alert than she had anticipated. If his health allowed, he would grow into a highly intelligent man — providing he had the right teachers, of course. And here she felt she had a great responsibility. After a light lunch they returned to the rose garden at the side of the old house, one area that was still reasonably looked after, and went on with the boy's studies. She had selected history as one of the afternoon's subjects, and it was during this work that they considered ancient Egypt.

"My father knows a lot about Egypt," Richard said proudly as he sat on the marble bench beside her in the warm sunshine.

"I'm sure he does," Sarah agreed.

"He studies about it all the time," Richard continued. "And he has a lot of things stored up in the attic that he had sent from Egypt."

"Really?" Sarah said. "They must be interesting. Perhaps we could get him to show us some of them. It would make your study of the land more enjoyable."

Richard considered this, a doubtful expression on his small, pale face framed by the yellow hair. "I don't think so," he decided.

"Why not?"

"Because they are mysterious things," he said, his blue eyes large with boyish intrigue.

"Oh?"

"My mummy didn't like having them up there," Richard went on. "She used to worry about it when she was sick. She seemed unhappy most all the time."

"That was natural because she was so ill," Sarah said, placing an arm around him.

Richard frowned in remembrance. "She told my father she didn't want the crates with the dead people's bodies in them opened. She said they were bound to bring a curse on the house."

Sarah was vaguely uneasy at the turn the conversation was taking. She tried to dismiss the subject lightly, saying, "It could be that among your father's Egyptian specimens there are some ancient embalmed bodies. The Egyptians were skilled in mummifying their dead and preserving them in ornamental stone coffins. We call that kind of coffin a sarcophagus."

"That is what I think my father has up there in the attic," Richard assured her.

"We must ask him," she said.

The lad looked frightened. "No, you mustn't!" he warned her. "He doesn't like to talk about the things he has in the attic."

She stared at him. "Are you sure?"

"Yes." Richard nodded his head vigorously. "He doesn't like to mention them to anyone, except Abigail maybe."

"You think he talks to Abigail about them?"

Richard nodded solemnly. "Yes. When Mummy was sick I heard him and Abigail whispering in the hall outside her door. My father said he had made a great discovery. And he said he knew as much as any man alive about Egypt's ancient poisons."

6

Unwittingly the child had brought a shadow of horror to the pleasant afternoon. Sarah pretended not to be upset by his remark. By turning to the lessons again, she managed to maintain an appearance of calm and finish the work she had outlined for Richard that day.

At four o'clock she closed the last book, and with a smile for Richard, said, "That's all for today. Now you must go to your room and rest, as Dr. Gideon said."

Richard stood up with a fretting expression. "He's a silly old man. I hate that stuffy room!"

"Your father insists you do as the doctor says," she pointed out. "And I don't want him to be angry with us for disobeying him. You go up to your room for a while, and perhaps we can take a walk after dinner. Wouldn't you like that?"

"Oh, yes! I want to," the boy said, smiling.

"Then run along," Sarah told him. "And we'll meet after dinner."

She watched as he ran into the old house by a side door, then, with a sigh, she stacked the books beside her on the marble bench. She let her gaze wander across the lawn to one of the statues, and considered what the boy had revealed to her.

John Stone had been whispering to Abigail concerning poisons outside the door of his ailing wife's room. Richard had not been aware of the import of his remark. But Sarah could not help being horrified at the thought that the villagers might be right after all! That John had conspired to take his wife's life with some long-forgotten poison he had uncovered in the work among his Egyptian relics in the attic.

Had the master of Dankhurst and the demure Abigail rid themselves of the unfortunate Penelope so they might marry when the scandal died down! It seemed more than a possibility and confirmed all the doubts she'd had about the quiet Abigail Durmot. She was more certain than ever that Abigail was playing a role, cleverly pretending to be a demure innocent when she was probably just the opposite. And Abigail's declaration of her interest in Rodney rather than John lacked subtlety.

She had been too anxious to make a point of it. Just as she had gone out of her way to fill Sarah with stories of the jealous ghost of a dead Priscilla Kirk out to completely possess John Stone.

Recalling vividly the attack on her the previous night, Sarah felt her anger rise. That fantasy about Priscilla Kirk had been told her only to confuse her, to make her blind to what was really going on around her. She was certain she had been brought to the estate for a purpose, but she could not yet decide what it might be. Certainly she was meant to be a pawn in a game in which the rules were unknown to her and in which she could not yet ascertain the motives of the chief players.

Her eyes glazed with tears. When she had seen the handsome John Stone studying her sympathetically in the courtroom in Edinbugh she had felt he might be her knight in shining armor, the man who had come to save her. And when the judge had turned her over to his care she had still hoped this might be the case. But the judge's second thoughts on the matter had turned out to be only too true. She had been betrayed by the jealousy of Amelia Gordon and the innocent kindness her ineffectual husband had attempted to offer her, and now she faced a second betrayal, in a different manner and for another motive!

She would write the judge a note and hope that it reached him and that he acted on it quickly. In the meantime she searched her mind to try and think of one friend she might have at Dankhurst, one person whom she could trust. . . . There was only one possibility: Rodney Stone.

Though it was true he was a rebel and given to carousing, she felt he had a basic honesty and a kind heart. She was sure that if anyone in the old mansion could be trusted, Rodney was that person. And she determined to consult him about her suspicions and fears. She would also reveal to him the attack that had been made on her the previous night.

She stood up with the books to start toward the house when the tall crone, Mrs. Fergus, came marching out of the house toward her. The nut-brown, wrinkled face of the old woman bore its usual dour expression.

Coming over to Sarah, she said, "The master would like to see you in his study."

"Thank you," Sarah said quietly. "I was just going in. Isn't it lovely out here?"

Mrs. Fergus scowled. "Not like it was in

Mrs. Stone's day. She kept the grounds looking like an enchanted garden."

"You were very devoted to her," Sarah said.

The old woman nodded her gray head. "Mistress Penelope was like my own bairn."

"I can imagine how sad you felt when she was taken," Sarah went on. "Yet it could not have been unexpected if she'd always been sickly, like poor little Richard."

Mrs. Fergus glared at her. "My Penelope were a bonny lass when she first came here!"

"I'm sorry," Sarah said, taken aback. "I didn't know."

"It was only after she saw this cursed spot she began to ail," the old woman went on darkly. Again Sarah felt her suspicions rising.

Probing to learn more, she ventured, "Then this was a sudden ailment that struck her down?"

"It was no normal sickness," Mrs. Fergus said, her wrinkled face convulsed with hate. "He knows that."

"You mean Mr. John?"

The old woman made no direct answer, her eyes slitted against the sun as she stared out across the lawn. "He brought the curse on this house! With his heathen goings-on up there. She tried to warn him, begged him to listen to her; but he wouldn't."

"You're talking about his Egyptian research and the relics he has up there," Sarah said. "Penelope didn't approve of them?"

"A bonny lass until he changed it all," the old woman muttered. And then she glared at Sarah. "You will find out soon enough!"

Sarah was alarmed at her sudden attack. "What do you mean?"

Mrs. Fergus gave a harsh cackle. "Your brazen pretty face will never match my Penelope's. And however much you cater to her bairn, you will never take her place in this house."

She gasped. "I have no idea of attempting that."

The old woman nodded. "You will find out about the attic soon enough."

"What about the attic?"

Mrs. Fergus gave another cackle. "Ask Priscilla Kirk!" And she turned and walked back to the house.

Sarah stared at her retreating back. The conversation had been less than satisfactory. Why had the old woman referred to the mansion's legendary ghost in that fashion? What had she meant? Or was her talk merely the incoherent ramblings of a senile mind.

Yet she had learned something from the old housekeeper. Penelope had not suffered from any chronic illness until she came to Dankhurst. And her fatal attack had come on rather suddenly. It fitted in with the growing feeling Sarah had that Abigail and John were responsible for his wife's death.

So John Stone was waiting to see her now, she thought grimly. What would this man who never smiled have to say this time? Would he lay down some new rules for young Richard's care? Give strict instructions as to how she was to conduct his lessons? She walked toward the house and the waiting John Stone. And afterward she meant to write the judge and tell him of her plight. She was certain he would arrange for her to return to Edinburgh, but even that worried her, for it would mean deserting the boy for whom she was beginning to feel true affection.

The house was cool and shadowed after her long sojourn in the sun. She put the books down and went along the corridor to John Stone's study. Finding the door ajar, she tapped on it gently and entered at his bidding.

He rose from his cluttered desk and waved her to a chair in the book-lined room. "I watched you and Richard as you worked," he said. "You seemed to be getting along very well."

"He is a bright boy."

John nodded his approval. "I feel the same way. Yet I do not want his frail constitution burdened with too many studies. I wanted to warn you about that, so I sent Mrs. Fergus out to fetch you."

"I will not overtax him," she promised.

"Excellent," he said, and remained standing behind the broad desk as if something were troubling him. "If I haven't already warned you about Mrs. Fergus, let me do it now. She is not entirely sane."

Sarah raised her eyebrows. "I noticed her manner was a little odd. But I did not think her mad."

"Close to it." He sighed. "She's a very old woman, although she has surprising physical strength for one her age. She was my late wife's maid before Penelope married me. And of course she is very devoted to her memory. In fact I believe Penelope's death triggered her madness."

"I see."

"She is apt to ramble or perhaps ignore words spoken to her altogether," he went on. "And sometimes she makes quite ridiculous accusations. And statements that are sheer fantasy."

"I believe she resents me," Sarah confessed. "She does not have much to say to me."

"She resents anyone new in the house," John Stone assured her. "Do not be disturbed by her attitude or by anything she may say."

"Thank you for explaining," she said.

He stood there rather unhappily. And she wondered if he thought she suspected something and was doing his best to put her at her ease. Was he worried about her becoming aware of what went on in the house too soon?

He said, "How are you today? I didn't have a chance to ask this morning."

"Very well."

"You are not suffering from your experience of last night?" he asked, his eyes searching out hers. "Your nightmare passed?"

"Yes. I went right to sleep after I talked to you."

"When I heard your screams I thought you were in some sort of danger."

She forced a smile, thinking that if he and Abigail were playing a game with her, they were acting their parts very well. "I fear I made myself seem a typical hysterical female to you."

"No harm was done," he said evenly, "so long as your mind is at rest now."

"You need not worry about me."

"I'm glad to know you are fully yourself again," he said. "We'll dwell no more on the subject. The main thing is that Richard likes you."

She smiled. "And I am drawn to him."

John Stone frowned. "He needs affection, and I regret that I have been in no fit frame of mind to offer it."

"But surely you should make yourself lavish affection on the boy."

He stared down at his desk top. "I have been deep in a most important phase of my research work. When I have cleared some of it away I fully plan to give him more attention."

"I hope you will find the time soon," she declared.

"I will try," he assured her. "And thank you for giving me these few minutes."

She rose with a polite smile. "I consider it part of my duties to hold counsel with you occasionally."

"And I agree," he said, walking with her to the door. "I trust you are not too disappointed with Dankhurst."

She hesitated at the door. "It is rather different from what I expected."

"In what way?"

"It is perhaps more remote," she said. "Until recently I have known only the city."

"Never mind," he said. "I will try to make it pleasant for you here. Although you have taken this position, do not think my sympathy for you is any less."

"Thank you," she said quietly.

"I am well aware of the ordeal you have recently undergone," he continued. "And I believe the quiet of the country will help restore your health. Meanwhile, an occasional nightmare such as you had last night is quite understandable."

"You are too kind," she said.

"Not at all. Look on this as your own home," John told her. "And if you find me abrupt or difficult in any way, merely put it down to my own unhappiness."

"I will," she said.

His eyes met hers. "We must talk again. There are so many things we have not had time to discuss. I would enjoy learning more about you and your past. We are little more than strangers, yet I hope you know with what sincerity I am your true friend."

"I am well aware of that," she said demurely.

137

She left him with mixed emotions. In fact she was so confused that she almost missed the rustle of a skirt that betrayed the presence of someone who had been listening to her talk with John from a dark corner below the stairway. Sarah halted at the sound, and peering into the shadows, saw Abigail Durmot standing there.

"You startled me," Sarah said.

The quiet girl emerged from the darkness to stand facing her with an odd, sullen look on her attractive face. "I didn't mean to," she said in her quiet fashion. "I was putting some things in a closet under there."

"I see."

"You'll excuse me." Abigail hurried past her and down the corridor.

Sarah was sure Abigail was in a rage, that she had overheard John's friendly words to Sarah and was suffering a fit of jealousy. If the two were joined in an evil alliance, Abigail would probably lose no time visiting him in his study and upbraiding him for his conduct. Sarah gave a weary sigh, and then went upstairs.

In her own room she stood by the window looking down at the courtyard and trying to puzzle it all out in her own mind. Just now John Stone had seemed quite different from his usual dour self. He had almost convinced her that she was wrong in her suspicions concerning him and Abigail. Then she had come upon the girl lurking in the shadows, eavesdropping on them, and her suspicions were again aroused.

Staring at the idle fountain and the stagnant lily pond circling it, Sarah was reminded of the terrifying moment last night when she had looked at the reflection of herself and John in the water only to see a third face there. The hideous face with hatred written on it! What had it meant? Had it been a ghostly portent of things to come? A warning to her?

She was about to sit down and compose the letter to the judge when she heard sounds from above — a scurrying of feet and a door slamming. It came from the same section as the sounds of the previous night — the area John had assured her was given over to storage space.

She stood looking at the ceiling and waited to hear more. But there was only silence now. It seemed that at least several people in the old mansion felt all the evil came from that attic area. John had brought all his imported relics from the Nile to those attic rooms and apparently spent a great deal of time up there studying them. What dark secret of the ancient past could he have come upon?

Why had his nature suddenly changed? Was it, as many thought, because he felt a guilt in the death of his sister in that disastrous fire, or was it because he was carrying on an illicit romance with his wife's cousin Abigail and had murdered his wife to further this plan?

Sarah was suddenly filled with a curiosity to visit the attic. She knew there was a short stairway leading to it at either end of the old house. There was time to go up now before she began to dress for dinner. And who knew what answer to the puzzle might be revealed up there.

Her mind made up, she quickly left her room and furtively made her way down the hall until she came to the narrow wooden steps that led to the upper regions. The steps were steep and creaked with age.

When she reached the attic level she saw that the windows along the outside corridor were grimy and spiders had spun their silken webs across the frames. She moved down the narrow corridor with its many doors. The wooden floor was bare, and her every step produced a slight groan from it. She tried to estimate when she was directly over her own room, and noted there was a door in the region. Probably the door she had heard slammed on those few occasions.

Now she hesitated, caught between curiosity and outright fear. She wanted to try the door and see where it might lead to and what she might discover behind it, but she also was afraid of what she might find. Perhaps some undreamed of horror!

While she stood there debating with herself a creak of the floorboards behind her filled her with terror. She stood frozen, unable to turn and face whatever might be there. Almost nauseated with fear, she waited for what seemed an interminable time before she gathered the courage to wheel around and see that there was no sign of anyone. It must have been an overwrought imagination that had made her so sure she'd heard a footstep.

With her courage returning, she advanced to the door and tried the knob. To her surprise, it turned under the pressure of her hand, and she was able to gently push the door open. Her first reaction was to note the smell of musty age that came from the darkened room. She opened the door a little farther and took a step inside.

The light that entered from the corridor allowed her a limited view of the room and its contents. There were large cartons on the floor of the shadowed room, mostly stout wooden ones, some of them opened and some nailed shut. There were several long ones that looked like coffins; then, finally, she saw the gray stone sarcophagus resting upright against the wall. It was decorated with the face and body of an Egyptian of the period. So this was John Stone's collection of Egyptian relics, or at least a part of them.

This must be a storage room, as she saw no desk or chair for his use. Probably some other attic room was reserved for his workroom, or he might even take some of the smaller items down to his study. Again she scanned the boxes and uttered a tiny gasp as she saw something small and black creep across one of them. Her immediate thought was a scorpion, and she took a hurried step back in dismay. In doing so she bumped against the cold stone of the sarcophagus and gave herself another fright.

Ready to retreat from the eerie room with its exotic contents, she gave the sarcophagus a final glance, and to her utter horror she saw its cover slowly opening. She froze there in sheer disbelief. Then, when it was one-third open a thin, grimy hand was showing, she gave a terrified cry and fled the room. She heard footsteps; then someone grasped her roughly from behind. The smell of musty age was overwhelming! She fainted. . . .

When she opened her eyes John Stone was bending over her. She raised herself on her elbow with a frightened gasp and he put an arm around her and gently helped her to her feet.

"You were on the floor in a faint when I came up here," he said.

Swaying a little she stared up at him. "Something came after me!"

He frowned. "Came after you?"

"Yes. It was close behind me. I could smell this awful odor, and then it took hold of me, and I fainted."

John looked incredulous. "I'm not sure I know what you're talking about," he said. "What were you doing up here?"

She hesitated before replying. Unable to link her visit to the attic with what had happened the previous night, she said, "I thought I'd like to see this part of the house. I felt the view might be interesting from up here."

"But I told you the attic was used only for storage. That no one comes up here except myself," he said sternly. "I do not

143

want people coming up here."

"I didn't understand," she said in a weak voice.

"Then you do now," he went on, his face grim. "I have a great many extremely valuable pieces up here. Some of them not even uncrated. I cannot risk their being stolen or tampered with by servants, or even by guests and members of the household. So I have made a strict rule that the attic is out of bounds."

"You need not worry about my coming up here again."

He sighed. "I hope you will not add to the nonsense that is already being spread about this place. Because I have ruled that no one can come up here, the servants tell a wild tale about the attic being haunted by the ghost of Priscilla Kirk."

Sarah, gradually regaining her poise, saw that John was nervous, as well as badly upset. Finding her up in his private domain had angered him. Yet he was trying vainly to placate her so she would not speak of her terrifying experience to anyone else.

She said, "I went in a room with a lot of crates and a sarcophagus standing against the wall."

He nodded. "Well?"

"While I was standing there the sarcophagus lid began to open. I saw an emaciated, dirty hand!"

He shook his head. "Your nerves are still not in a normal state."

"You mean I didn't see that stone coffin gradually opening?"

"I'm afraid not," he said. "The coffin is empty."

She shook her head. "No. There was something inside it. Something that came out of it and tried to hold me back."

"Pure imagination!" he said. "I'll show you the sarcophagus and prove it is empty, if you like."

"No," she said. "I'd rather not!"

He seemed distressed by her assertion. "I don't know of any other way to convince you," he said.

"Please; I'd rather forget all about it."

He nodded. "Perhaps that would be best. I'll see you safely downstairs. And I will ask your promise not to come up here again."

"I have no intention of it," she assured him.

He followed her down the narrow stairs. "And again, I'll ask you not to say anything to the others. I'm sure you conjured up all that you told me out of a moving shadow and your imagination."

"No, I cannot agree with that," she said, the memory of that awful moment still vivid in her mind.

John was walking her to the door. "Then think what you will, but do not say anything," he begged. "This I ask of you. We have had enough trouble with wild rumors in this house as it is."

"I will not mention it," she promised.

He paused at the door. "And under no circumstances go up there again," he reminded her.

In her room she began to change for dinner. And now she wondered how it happened that John Stone was so promptly on the scene after her faint. Had his sudden appearance scared off the horrible thing that had pursued her? Or had he been instrumental in sending whatever it was away?

The shock of the encounter still made her feel weak. And she no longer doubted that John Stone had some dark secret concealed in that attic, something that had a bearing on all that had happened at Dankhurst.

She put on a white dress for dinner and went down to join the others in the big dining room. Seeing Rodney there gave her spirits a needed lift, and he was his usual jovial self as he helped her with her chair. She sat on one side of the poet, and the youngster, Richard, on the other.

"Miss Bennett is going to take me for a walk after dinner," Richard said, his face all smiles.

Rodney gave her a wink. "How lucky you are, Richard. I only wish she would do the same for me."

From the head of the table, John frowned. "I'm not sure the night air will be good for the boy."

"It will barely be sunset," Rodney said, coming to Richard's defense. "I can't see that it will do him any harm."

"But then you are not a physician, are you?" John's tone was sarcastic.

"Nor is that fossil you drag here from Rawlwyn," Rodney said drily.

"We are not going to argue the merits of Dr. Gideon," John said with some anger.

"Obviously not" — Rodney chuckled — "since he has none."

To settle the awkward moment, Sarah spoke up quickly. "I promise I will not keep Richard out too long."

Richard prattled happily with Rodney about his lessons while John contented himself with scowling at his brother from time to time. Abigail Durmot eyed Sarah's dress with envy — her plain brown taffeta looked drab by comparison — and all through the meal she said little, and then only to John.

Sarah was glad to get away from the stiff atmosphere of the table and take Richard by a small hand to lead him out across the lawns for a final walk of the day. The sun was beginning to set, but the air was still pleasant.

"Can we do this every night after dinner?" the blond boy wanted to know.

"We'll see," she said. "It depends on the weather."

"I've been waiting for this all afternoon," he said with the seriousness of a grown-up. "I like you, Miss Bennett. Please, must I call you Miss Bennett?"

She smiled. "Only when your father and the others are around. I don't mind your calling me Sarah when we are alone. But not otherwise, or they'll think I'm being neglectful of your manners."

"Yes, Sarah," the boy said. "I like that name." They had come up to one of the statues, and Richard paused to stare at it. "My great-grandfather had these made and put out here. They are all likenesses of his friends and family."

148

"So I understand," Sarah said, studying the plaster effigy of a grim old man who glared at her in a startling, lifelike fashion.

"That is Squire McCallum," Richard said. "I know most of them by name. My mummy taught me."

Richard tugged at her hand and led her down a small slope, excited in his desire to give her a complete tour of the statuary. Ahead was the plaster effigy of a maiden dressed in the quaint bonnet and gown of that long-ago period.

Sarah laughed. "Slowly, or I'll stumble on this uneven ground!"

Richard brought her close to the statue. "This one is scarred by the weather," he said, "but she was a very famous lady, my mummy told me. Her name was Priscilla Kirk."

His words caught her by surprise, and she found herself staring at the statue. It was true the weather had taken its toll of the dainty figure. The face was marred, with the nose mutilated and great holes in the cheeks, so that instead of being placidly beautiful the plaster features bore a grotesquely ugly look. Sarah gave a small shudder. It was almost the identical face she had seen reflected in the pond the previous night.

7

The illusion, for only such could Sarah believe it to be, held her for a long moment. Then she forced herself to turn away from the mutilated face. Even then she knew its image, along with that of the one she'd seen on the surface of the pond, would continue to haunt her.

"She isn't a very beautiful lady now, is she?" Richard asked.

"No, I'm afraid not," she said quietly, and they began to walk on.

"You are beautiful," Richard said.

She smiled down at him. "And you are a young gallant for your age," she said. "I shall have to watch my step with you."

"When I own all this I would like a beautiful lady like you for my wife," the little boy said solemnly. "Will you wait for me, Sarah?"

She sighed. "I think I would like that very much indeed. But I'm sure you would be disappointed. By that time I'd be old and look like Mrs. Fergus."

"Not ever!" the boy said stoutly.

They strolled on across the wide lawns and Sarah, aware of the neglect of the once carefully tended grounds, felt it was a pity John was allowing the estate to fall into such a condition. Little Richard was busy giving her the names of the various plaster figures as they came to them. It took more than a half hour, and then it was time to take him back to the house and see him to his bed.

"This was my best day since my mummy was alive," the boy said from his pillow. "Don't ever leave, Sarah."

She gave him a gentle smile. "Not for a long time anyway." And she bent down and kissed him good night.

It wasn't until after she'd left the forlorn youngster in the shadowed room that she realized she was trapped — a prisoner of a lovable yellow-haired boy. It would be senseless to write to the judge now and ask that he help her return to Edinburgh. She would not leave Richard until she was certain the boy was in no danger.

But she did want to have a talk with Rodney Stone as she had planned. And this was more urgent than ever, now that she had made up her mind to remain at Dankhurst for at least a little while. She made her way downstairs and saw no one. The great house seemed deserted. She supposed John Stone was off somewhere buried in his research, and Abigail Durmot was possibly in her room.

Rodney had joked about wanting to take a walk with her, so now she went outside again. Dusk was beginning to fall and the air had more of a chill; still, she was not cold. She stood on the porch a moment, and then she saw Rodney strolling up the gravel walk and went out to meet him.

He greeted her with a smile on his handsome face. "Well, I am indeed in luck. I was just about to abandon myself to despair and the tavern in Rawlwyn village when you show up."

Returning his smile, she said, "I've been wanting to talk to you."

"Now that is a very good sign," he said with mock seriousness. "If we nurture your feelings carefully they may blossom into true love!"

"Please don't make fun of me," she pleaded. "I need someone, and I believe you are the only person here I can completely trust."

"You do me honor, Miss Bennett."

"Sarah will suffice if we are to be friends," she said.

"And I shall be Rod to you," he told her. And taking her by the arm, he guided her away from the house. "There is a marble bench a short distance from here, suitably concealed by hedges. It offers privacy and cuts off the view of these devilish gargoyles that mar our lawn."

She laughed. "Richard is quite fond of them. He knows them all by name."

"He will outgrow the weakness," Rodney predicted.

When they were seated she began to tell him of her experience of the night before, and its sequel that afternoon. Rodney listened with an expression of disbelief.

"The devil you say!" was his astonished comment when she finished her recital.

It was almost dark now, and she stared at him earnestly. "I know my story sounds much like the invention of a madwoman, but I swear all I have told you is solemn truth."

"I'm not about to deny it," Rodney said. "It is no secret to me that the house is the scene of some black doings."

"Do you have any idea what it all means?"

"I wish I did," he said in a worried voice. "Sometimes I have strange suspicions, and then I discover I am wrong." He paused. "Certainly John is not in any way the man he once was."

"You mean before Penelope's death?"

"Even longer ago than that," he said in a sad voice. "Our best days, the happiest days I vow that Dankhurst knew, was when we three were growing up."

"You three?"

"Yes. John and Justine and I. John was half brother to both of us, but we were so close there was no difference at all." He paused. "It was our very happiness that brought tragedy in the end. Justine cared more for John than a half-sister should. And I think she would have been content to spend her days here a spinster and the mistress of his household. She had a mad affection for him — an affection that swiftly turned to hatred when John brought Penelope here as his bride."

"Your sister did not remain here long after that?"

"No. That autumn she met the Frenchman, and she left in the night without so much as a note. The next we heard was from someone who met her in a village outside Paris. She was married, and they were living there in a cottage. But she wasn't happy — or so this person said. Later came the news of the fire and her being burned to death, along with her husband. John was shocked, and he had one of his few serious quarrels with Penelope. He blamed her for driving his sister away and to her death."

"Which wasn't true!" Sarah said.

"Of course not," Rodney agreed. "Justine was my sister, but I could not blame Penelope because I knew it was Justine who was to blame. But after her death she became a kind of martyr in John's mind."

"That was when he began to brood and neglect the estate?"

"He returned when I was away in London. When I came back Penelope took me aside and whispered her fears about him. She told me that he had been furtive and moody since his return from France and had taken to burying himself for long hours in his study. He also had brought back a number of strange objects with him that had recently been unearthed by an archaeological expedition in Egypt."

"That was before Penelope became ill?"

"Yes," Rodney said in a strained voice. "But I believe his turning his back on her had something to do with her illness. That, as well as the curse those scavengings from an Egyptian tomb brought to the house."

"You are superstitious about them?"

"I think the buried dead should be allowed to stay in their graves," Rodney said darkly. "John and his fellows engaged in this study maintain they are students of history. I say they are little better than grave robbers! And the curse that damns all such ghouls is upon them."

"So much for John," she said. "You put it down to his guilty feelings concerning Justine's death, his interest in archaeology, and above all, his added unhappiness over Penelope's death that has crushed his spirit."

"And his obsession with the legend of Priscilla Kirk," Rodney reminded her. "Also his sudden interest in poisons."

"Has it ever occurred to you his interest in poisons may have something in common with his studies of ancient Egypt? They developed some of the most virulent and subtle poisons. Perhaps he found some of them among his discoveries, or at least the formulas to make them."

She could not make out Rodney's features clearly in the darkness now, but she could tell that her words had upset him by the way he suddenly became silent.

After a moment, he said, "What are you suggesting?"

"I'm going to ask you a very frank question. Do you mind?"

He gave a small laugh. "Well, at least I have fair warning."

"Is Abigail Durmot in love with you?"

"Not that I'm aware of," he said quickly.

"Are you in love with her?"

"To that, the answer must be another no," he said. "Why do you ask me such questions?"

"Because she led me to believe there was a romance between you two."

"The minx! I'll be having a word with her about that," Rodney sputtered.

"I wish you wouldn't," Sarah begged. "I don't want to put her on her guard. I knew she told me the story to confuse me about her and John."

"Ah!" Rodney said. "You think there is fire between those two?"

"I suspect it. And more."

"More?"

"Because of what I have heard from the boy," she said. And she repeated what Richard had said about hearing his father and Abigail whispering about poison outside his dying mother's room.

"I don't like the sound of it!" Rodney announced dramatically. "I fear those two have been up to no good."

"It is only a child's story," she reminded him. "I may be wrong or making too much of nothing. But I had to confide in someone."

"I am heartily glad you have," he said. "And though I can't see John as a wife poisoner, I must agree the facts look black against him. And Abigail!"

"I am puzzled by Abigail Durmot," Sarah confessed. "Is she truly such a meek creature? And such a quiet mouse when it comes to men?"

Rodney chuckled softly. "Your suspicions are well-founded. She is not what she appears to be. And from my own knowledge, I can tell you she is not averse to the arms of a male."

"Ah!" Sarah said accusingly. "So there is something between you two!"

"Nothing of consequence; that I can promise you," Rodney asserted. "She is far too shallow for my taste. But I wanted to let you know you have guessed the truth about her."

"So she could be capable of plotting to rid John of his wife?"

"Aye, I must admit it."

"They may have killed Penelope and now be ready for another victim," Sarah said. "I do believe that is why I was brought here. John saw that he could make use of me because I escaped my trial with the shady reputation of being a possible poisoner."

"How would that benefit him?"

"I could be a scapegoat at the proper time. Someone to blame for a second murder those two may be contemplating."

Rodney gave a low whistle. "It is a logical thought, but I can't bring myself to see my half brother so diabolical a man, even with an evil woman to nudge him on, nor can I picture him as a multiple murderer."

"I see," she said quietly. "You find it easier to cling to a belief in the curse of the ancient Egyptians, or perhaps the vengeful haunting of Priscilla Kirk? It seems you are left with a choice."

"Make light if you will," Rodney said solemnly, "but there may be more to those things than you can guess."

"I'm not so afraid of the dead as I am of the living," Sarah said. "I fear your brother has become a madman, and I think he will next strike at his own little son. To remove that link with the woman he murdered."

"No!" Rodney said loudly. "He would not harm Richard!"

"I tell you I have real fear for the child," Sarah assured him. "And why does he insist on having that doctor in his dotage look after the boy as he looked after Penelope?"

"I have fought him about that."

"And it has done no good," Sarah said bitterly. "Let me tell you why. Because with Dr. Gideon, there is no fear of his being revealed as a poisoner."

Rodney slapped a fist in his open palm. "By the heavens, it does fit! What are we to do about it?"

"I'm afraid nothing until we are more certain of our facts than we are now," Sarah said calmly. "I think the attack was made on me to frighten me and convince me a ghostly figure does infest the house. To mix me up thoroughly so should I find myself trapped in a web of circumstance, I will babble wildly and help convict myself."

"If all you say is true, you are in very real danger," Rodney said with great earnestness.

"So is anyone else in the house who comes upon the truth, including you," Sarah pointed out. "I'm sorry to involve you, but I needed someone I could trust."

"And you decided on me," he said in a softer tone. "Rod, the poet and the sot."

"It seems you are truly neither," she said. "But best that John and Abigail think you are until all this is settled."

For answer, Rodney reached out and took her by the arms. "I have never had a hint of honest love for any female yet," he confessed. "But I believe there is a change since meeting you. I could fall in love with you, Sarah Bennett!"

"Until you took a fancy to the next pretty face," she chided him.

His grip on her arms grew tighter, until she almost winced. "No," he said. "I could be faithful to a girl like you." And he drew her close for an ardent kiss.

Sarah did not struggle to escape his embrace. Even though she did not feel she was in love with the reckless young man, she was very fond of him. And she counted on him now. She felt warm and protected in his arms. At last, with a deep sigh, he let her go.

"You suddenly seem sad," she told him.

He still held her hands in his, but now he shrugged and looked away into the darkness. "Even while I was kissing you a chill came over me. A sudden warning, as if from the grave. A nagging whisper that our love would never be!"

"I'm afraid my talk has filled you with strange fancies," she said.

Rodney gave a short bitter laugh. "Blame it on the poet in me," he suggested. "I am like Hamlet. I talk of love and all the while study the skull in my hand. I smell the odor of death about this place. And it frightens me that it could be your death or mine."

While he was speaking she had let her glance wander toward the old mansion. For there, on the attic level, a dull glow of lamplight had appeared at a window. She turned to Rodney. In a lowered voice, she said, "Look! In the attic! He must be up there now!"

"Brooding over his dead bodies," the poet said grimly. "Working at his sorcery and poisons. Up to some devilish mischief, you may be sure!"

"We could be doing him a great wrong. He may be innocent."

"Then there's a deal of explaining to be done that only ghosts could manage," Rodney said harshly. "No, little Sarah, you have presented too strong a case against my brother."

"You mustn't act rashly until we know for sure."

"And when will that be?" he demanded. "When he has finished both of us, along with Penelope, and the child as well?"

"I doubt if it will come to that," she said, rising. "I'm cold. Please take me back to the house."

They hurried back in the darkness. She

begged him to be patient, and he promised that he would. But she could tell that she had upset him badly with her theories; and with his impulsive nature, it would take a lot of self-control on his part to refrain from accusing his half brother openly. This was something she felt he must not do.

As they came onto the porch she turned and said to him, "Remember, you are not to rush at this in a frenzy. That way we are bound to fail."

He nodded, his face unusually pale. "I will try to remember."

"You must!" she insisted.

They went inside and up the dimly lighted stairway. At the door of her room he took her in his arms briefly and kissed her again. She was uneasy at the open manner in which he was professing his love for her, but trusted no prying eyes were watching them, though she couldn't be sure, recalling how Abigail had spied on her earlier.

After a final good night she entered her room and slid the bolt securely. The lamp was burning on her dresser, and she quickly prepared for bed. She felt reasonably secure behind the bolted door, and being able to talk freely to Rod had removed a great deal of her tension. She no longer felt she was carrying the burden of her fear alone. Rodney would be on the sidelines to watch and be ready to come to her assistance.

It was with this comforting thought that she fell asleep. Once again she woke in the darkness. And once again her sleep had been interrupted by sounds from the attic above. As she sat up in bed with the coverings clutched tightly to her, she heard a low moaning sound from the same area the noises had come the previous night. This time there was only a kind of weird soft wailing, and in a while it stopped altogether. She lay back on her pillow, her pretty face troubled, and she listened without hearing any other sound until sleep at last overtook her.

There was a change in the weather when she awoke in the morning. She could hear the downpour of rain even before she got out of bed. And when she went to the window she saw that it was teeming rain and the skies were a dark gray. It looked as if the storm would last the day.

She hurried through her morning toilet, anxious to get downstairs and have her breakfast so she could resume her work with Richard. She thought they might sit in the study and have a fire in the large

164

fireplace there. She would ask John for his permission. Surely he would give it. But you could never tell about the sober young man.

It was while she was descending the last flight of stairs that she heard the angry exchange between John and Rodney. She halted in fear of what might be said by the hot-tempered Rodney.

"I say you are daft or evil!" Rodney was telling his brother.

"And I suggest you keep your opinions to yourself," John said grimly.

"I warn you, if harm comes to Richard you'll answer to me!"

"He is my son!" John answered.

"More's the pity for him," was Rodney's hot reply, and he rushed out the front door and banged it after him.

John stood glaring angrily at the door as Sarah descended the remaining stairs and went across to him. "I didn't mean to eavesdrop," she said, "but I couldn't help hearing. What is wrong?"

John looked at her coldly. "Richard has taken a bad turn."

"Oh, no!"

"I was afraid you were overdoing things with him yesterday," he said in anger. "But you would not heed my warning."

"He seemed well and in good spirits when I put him to bed," she protested.

"And he has the fever and pains now," John snapped.

"There must be some other reason. It couldn't be the activity."

His eyes were furious. "So you must be both governess and doctor as well," he said. "You are a busybody, Miss Bennett. I can see that I was wrong in bringing you here."

"And I made a grave error in coming," she said hotly.

His face was stern. "I shall see to it that arrangements are made for you to leave."

"I would like to feel that Richard is out of danger before I go," she told him.

"What do you mean by out of danger?" he demanded.

She swallowed hard. "I simply meant that I would go feeling better if I knew his health had improved."

"Your concern is touching," John said with sarcasm.

"Have you sent for a doctor?" she asked.

"I have sent a message to Dr. Gideon. I'm certain he'll come as soon as he can. That was what my brother chose to argue with me about. He suggested I should have another doctor."

Sarah sighed. "It is not as if it were ground you haven't gone over before."

"The argument is an old one," he admitted. "But I will make the choice of my son's doctor. And my choice is Dr. Gideon."

"May I go up and see Richard?"

"I suggest you have your breakfast," he said. "Abigail is with him now. She has taken him up some gruel in the hope he will have a little. I do not wish him disturbed at the moment."

She lowered her head humbly. "As you say."

He cleared his throat. "I do not mean to be harsh. But I am concerned, and Rodney upset me just now."

"I fully understand," she said quietly, and moved on to the dining room.

She wasn't able to eat a proper breakfast. The food choked her.

Old Mrs. Fergus served her with a grim, satisfied expression on her brown wrinkled face. Sarah couldn't help feeling she had the look of a repulsive Highland witch.

As the old woman placed toast and a jar of marmalade on the table Sarah said, "Did you know Richard is ill?"

"I knew it before most!" the old woman said.

"I can't imagine what's wrong."

The old woman busied herself with the teapot. "Could be the lack of a mother's love," she snapped. "Or the attempt of some, who should know better, to replace it."

Sarah looked at her. "Are you referring to me? I only tried to help Richard yesterday. I'm truly fond of the boy."

The old woman scowled. "He will die just as she did."

"You mustn't say such things!"

"It will happen! Old Dr. Gideon will come and shake his head, just as he did over my Miss Penelope. And the evil will kill the lad, same as it took her from us."

Sarah regarded her with alarm, about to make a protest. Then she recalled that John had warned her the old woman was slightly mad, and it would be futile to try and reason with her.

So she said simply, "I hope you are proven wrong, Mrs. Fergus."

"I know what I know," the old woman said darkly, and went on out to the kitchen.

Sarah drank her tea, then went back to the hallway. She hadn't been there more than a moment when she saw Abigail coming down with a dish in her hands.

Sarah asked, "Was he able to take any of the gruel?"

Abigail looked very pale. She shook her head. "Hardly any. He seems sick to his stomach and he has severe pains."

"Well, that surely can't be the result of my keeping him out in the air and taking him for a walk," she said.

Abigail was at the foot of the stairs now. In her demure way she said, "He seems overtaxed." It was as if to say that Sarah was to blame for tiring him beyond his strength.

"I'd hardly diagnose that from his symptoms," Sarah said. "It sounds more like a case of food poisoning to me."

Abigail's eyes met hers in an unflinching gaze. She said, "But then you would know more about that than the rest of us."

Sarah had an angry retort on her lips, but she clenched her hands and forced herself to remain silent. It was well that she did, because at that moment John Stone came out to join them. He asked Abigail if his son had been able to eat and received the same negative reply.

John sighed and said, "Well, at least you have done your best."

Abigail suggested, "Perhaps a little later on he may take some broth."

"It might be well to wait until after the doctor comes," John said in a worried voice.

Abigail went out the hallway in the direction of the kitchen, leaving John and Sarah standing at the foot of the stairs alone. Neither glanced at the other for a moment; both were tense.

Sarah was quickly putting two and two together. From what she had heard, Richard must have eaten something that had upset him, or worse still, somebody might have deliberately given him some sort of poison. She wondered what the boy had eaten and felt sure if she had a talk with him she would be able to trace the source of his illness. There was little hope Dr. Gideon would manage this. So it would be up to her.

She turned to John. "May I please go up to him now? He will wonder at my not coming."

He gave her an uneasy glance. "There's no question of his doing any studies today."

"I know that. I just want to talk to him."

"It would be well for him to rest until Dr. Gideon gets here."

She said, "I promise not to disturb him. I only ask a few minutes to let him know

I'm sorry he's ill and that I'll be here to help him with his work when he is better."

John Stone shrugged with resignation. "Since you insist," he said. "But I don't want you to remain with him more than five minutes at the most."

"I won't," she said.

The darkened room had an odor of sickness that assailed her nostrils at once and made her more concerned than ever. The boy had apparently been throwing up and was running a high fever. She went quickly to his bedside, and her heart filled with pity as she looked down at the flushed, tormented face.

Richard opened his eyes and his little face brightened. He whispered, "Sarah!"

She reached out and took his perspiring hand. "It's all right. You're going to be better soon."

"You promise?"

"I promise.

"My tummy hurts and I threw up in the night," he said plaintively.

"Richard, I can only stay a minute before the doctor comes so I want you to think quickly," she said. "Tell me what you've eaten since yesterday afternoon."

"Everything?" he asked, wide-eyed.

"Everything."

He slowly began to recite what he had had for dinner. It was food they had all shared and she eliminated any possibility of poisoning there. Then he mentioned that Abigail had brought a cup of hot cocoa before he went to sleep. Sarah's heart began to pound faster. The cocoa!

Then his weak little voice broke into her thoughts by adding, "And my mummy came to see me again in the middle of the night."

A chill ran down Sarah's spine. "You just imagined that. You dreamed it in your fever."

Richard shook his head on the pillow. "No. She came and woke me up like she's done before. She was wearing a funny veil, and she told me she missed me and gave me a glass of something sweet that made me sleepy."

8

Sarah listened to the boy's story with fear and growing confusion. Surely this was some wild imagining of his fevered state. He now lay back on the pillow with his eyes closed, thoroughly exhausted.

Bending close to him, she asked, "What happened after you took the drink?"

He opened his eyes and gave her a weary glance. "I was sleepy and then I began to feel sick."

"Where is the glass?"

"My mummy took it back again when it was empty."

She stared at him not knowing what to think. He seemed able to fill in the details so completely. Children had vivid imaginations and were able to do that, she knew. He might be only repeating what he thought might have happened.

"And you've had nothing to eat since?"

"Not until Abigail brought me up some gruel. I wasn't able to keep any of it down.

My tummy hurts so!" And he turned away from her, a small hand on his stomach.

She touched his shoulder gently. "Just try and rest. The doctor will be here soon and he will give you something to make you feel better."

The boy gave no sign of having heard what she said or of her being there. She stood at his bedside a moment, feeling a deep frustration, then turned and left the room.

John was still pacing in the hallway as she descended the stairs. She studied him and wondered if his distress were real or feigned. Was he genuinely concerned about his ailing child upstairs, or was he a madman bent on completing a plan of murder? She couldn't decide. And the strange story Richard had told her did not help.

John stopped pacing to turn and give her his attention. His sober handsome face wore a questioning look, and it seemed to her there was misery in his eyes.

"Well?" he asked.

"I talked with him briefly," she said. "He seems to be suffering a good deal. I believe his stomach is upset from some bad food or drink."

He stared at her coldly. "Naturally you

174

would not put it down to his excessive energies of yesterday."

"I am only saying what I honestly think," she told him quietly.

His reply was to turn away from her and begin pacing again. She stood there at the bottom of the stairs, the hall damp and gray, the rain still beating a tattoo that could be plainly heard from the porch roof. After an awkward moment she went into the living room.

She found herself standing under the portrait of the unhappy Justine. The loveliness of the arrogant young woman's face shone out at her. John's half sister must have been a striking person, yet tainted with a kind of madness that had made her want to possess her handsome brother completely. Even Rodney, with all his charm, was by no means a stable man. So was it beyond possibility the family taint of insanity was driving John on to do horrible things?

Sarah stared at the wicked slash across the face of the canvas, and then her eyes wandered to the vacant place where Penelope's portrait was said to have hung. Abigail Durmot had been quick to tell her of the theory that it had been the jealous wraith of Priscilla Kirk who had mutilated

Justine's portrait and caused John Stone to remove the one of Penelope to protect it.

But she found it far easier to believe that Abigail herself might have slashed the painting in a fit of jealousy and persuaded John to remove his late wife's likeness for the same reason. This was on the assumption that the demure Abigail and the master of Dankhurst were collaborators in murder.

With a sigh she moved down the length of the shadowy depressing room to come to a halt before the fireplace and stare up at the portrait of old Stephen Dank who had built the great stone mansion so many years ago. He sat there glumly observing all that was happening, as he had since the artist caught him in this pose in his declining years. What would be his reaction to the strange events taking place at Dankhurst now? What would he think of its present master?

What, in fact, did she herself think of the handsome blond John Stone? And she knew that even under oath before a judge and jury, as she had so recently been, she would find it hard to present her views fairly. It caused her some shame to remember that in the beginning she had counted on him so, his understanding and sympathy had been extended to her generously, and she had looked upon him as her ideal of British manhood. Within her there had surely been the beginnings of love for him.

Yes, let her admit it so that it might be a lesson for all her life. She had felt that she could come to love John Stone and hoped that he would eventually come to profess some tender feelings for her. How it had all changed! And it began with her arrival at the old estate. It was then a new John Stone had been revealed to her. And she had begun to have serious doubts about her wisdom in coming to this isolated spot. John Stone, the obsessed student of Egyptian lore and the coldly, aloof parent, presented new facets of the man she thought she had known. Now it was all confusion and fear. She was beyond trying to sort it out, and she was anxious that the child she had grown to love should recover from his illness.

There was a violent pounding on the entrance door that caught her attention even in the living room. She turned with a puzzled look; then deciding it must herald the advent of the old physician, she hurried out to be there on his arrival.

John Stone opened the door to admit

Dr. Gideon, and a gust of rain and wind accompanied his entrance. Sarah thought she had never seen so odd a creature; in his bad-weather garb he resembled some monstrous character from a children's book illustration. On his octogenarian head was a broad-brimmed rubber hat such as seamen wore in a storm, and over his coat he had a great, flapping rubber cape.

There was much grunting and groaning on Dr. Gideon's part as John helped him divest himself of his outer layers of clothing. "Delayed by the weather," he mumbled. "Every year the storms get worse!"

"I'm sorry to have to bring you here on a day like this. But my boy seems so very ill."

The old man's parchment face took on a grave expression, and he nodded. Then turning to Sarah, with his bag grasped firmly in his hand, he peered at her nearsightedly and said, "Do not despair, Madam. I shall take care of your child."

Sarah watched him as he made his creeping ascent of the stairs. The old doctor's error, which might have had comic overtones under other circumstances, was frightening at this moment. John was accompanying the doctor, and she imagined he would stay with him until a diagnosis had been offered.

She resigned herself to another period of waiting. Glancing outside she saw that the doctor's carriage was in the driveway. The woebegone horse had a canvas covering thrown over it, and the youth who drove the rig was standing in the shelter of the porch. As she continued to peer out the window she heard a step in the hall behind her and turned to see Abigail.

The demure young woman seemed very uneasy. "The doctor is here?"

"Yes. He and Mr. Stone have gone up to Richard."

Abigail pressed her hands together nervously. "I do hope the report is encouraging. I have never seen the boy in such a state."

Sarah gave her a sharp glance. "It seems the attack came on with a strange suddenness."

Abigail turned away to gaze up the stairway. Sarah interpreted it as a device to avoid meeting her own accusing look. The attractive cousin of John Stone's late wife stood there without saying a word.

After a time there came a murmur of voices from above that gradually grew louder. John Stone's firm, troubled tone contrasted with the wheezy protestations of the old doctor. Then the two men appeared at the top of the stairs and made a slow descent.

Dr. Gideon paused before her and Abigail and offered them a feeble smile. "The lad will not suffer anymore," he said. "I have provided him with a tincture of opium to relieve his pain, and I have instructed his father when it is to be administered again."

Sarah was ready to brave John's anger by questioning the old doctor. "What do you think is the cause of his illness?" she asked.

The droopy, jowled face showed a puzzled expression. "I find it hard to name the cause of his indisposition, Madam." He waved an ancient hand vaguely. "The air is full of strange disorders, and a weak constitution is a gathering place for them."

Ignoring John Stone's outraged countenance and Abigail's shocked expression, she continued to question the doctor. "But surely this is some disorder of the stomach caused by bad food or drink?"

Dr. Gideon coughed and hunched his stooped shoulders. "You may have a strong point there, Madam!" he announced gravely. "I have known cases like this when the supply of drinking water was contaminated. It could be! It could be!"

"I'll help you with your things, Doctor,"

John said coming forward with the old man's cloak and ignoring Sarah altogether.

"Thank you, sir," the old man said happily. "The tincture of opium will do it. Have no fear!" And he struggled into the unwieldy cloak, clamped the rainhat on his bald head, and tottered to the door.

John Stone went out to see the doctor on his way, and Abigail vanished at the same time, hurrying off down the corridor that led to the rear of the old house. Sarah remained in the hallway, waiting for John to return. He did so after a moment. His head and shoulders showed signs of the downpour. He took a white linen handkerchief from his pocket and slowly dried the rivulets of rain from his face.

She met his gaze defiantly. "I suppose you are angry because I took it on myself to address the doctor."

"It wasn't your place to do it," he remarked quietly.

"I felt it my duty to the boy."

"And what did you accomplish, may I ask?"

"I made that silly old man admit at least one thing," she said angrily. "He agreed the boy could be the victim of some sort of poisoning."

"I didn't hear him say that. He mentioned the possibility of bad water."

"It amounts to the same thing," she insisted.

He gave her a strange glance. "I don't wish to discuss this any further here," he said. "Please come with me to my study."

She was puzzled by his sudden change of mood and slowly followed him down the corridor to his study. He waited for her to enter, then went in himself and closed the door. He went to the window and drew open the heavy drapes. The rain still streamed down on the panes of the tall windows.

He motioned her to a chair. "Please sit down," he said. "I want to clear up a few matters."

She did as he asked, and looking up at him, she tried to appear much calmer than she felt as she said, "Well?"

"You heard me arguing with my half brother this morning."

"I could not help hearing you."

"I understand that. The thing I wish to make clear is that we were having an argument about the medical treatment of my son."

"So?"

"You are questioning my actions in this matter in the same way?"

She shrugged. "Perhaps we are both of the same mind."

"I am certain of that," John said, standing before her, his face stern. "And I am not surprised, since it has come to my attention that you and Rodney spent some time together last evening."

Sarah blushed. "Is that not our business?"

"Not when you spend that time conspiring against me."

"That is not true!"

"Rodney's violent actions this morning and your own harsh words prove it," he said coolly.

"It is only the child's welfare we are thinking of."

"Even if that is so," he said, "I do not like this disloyalty on your part. I might have expected it from Rod."

"Your brother means you no harm."

"My half brother," he said coldly, "is a drunkard and profligate. I warned you against him before you were here a day."

"He has conducted himself well with me. I can say nothing against him," she replied with spirit. "I believe him to be my friend!"

A look of despair crossed John's face, and he turned to move across to the window. Looking back at her, he asked,

"And what of me? Are you determined that I be your enemy?"

"Not at all."

He stared at her from the window. "Then why have you changed so in your manner toward me?"

"I was not aware that I had."

He shook his head unhappily. "Now you know you are not telling me the truth. Why these evasions?"

Sarah hesitated, and then she boldly said, "If you must know, it is because of certain happenings in this house for which there seems no reasonable explanation. And because of your attitude toward your son in health and illness. If there must be further reasons: your odd obsession with those Nile relics, and your insistence on giving your time to them and neglecting all else."

He smiled grimly. "You make me sound like some sinister character. Is that what you think?"

"I have reserved any judgment."

"Thank you," he said with icy politeness. "You have given me a list of my shortcomings, but I doubt that you have troubled to make a like catalogue of my many problems."

"I do not wish to be unfair."

"Yet I think you are," he said, moving

across the room toward her. "You have forgotten the bereavements I have known, the nagging worry of a sickly son, my efforts to keep your precious Rodney out of trouble!"

Sarah's eyes met his. "I have not overlooked any of those things. And you can believe that when I first came here I was more than touched by your plight. But your refusal to even consider having another doctor for your son, when you must know Dr. Gideon was neglectful and incompetent in the instance of your wife's death, is more than I can tolerate or understand!"

He stood there staring silently as she ended her outburst. There was just the sound of the rain beating against the windows. At last he said in a grave voice, "If I agree to do as you say — call in another doctor — will you be convinced of my desire to do the right thing?"

She was startled by his offer. "Yes," she said. "I think so."

"Very well," he said "If the boy is not better in the morning I will call in another doctor from Rawlwyn — Dr. MacGregor, considered the best in the county."

"Why not call him at once?"

"I doubt if he would be available today. But I will send a message for him to come tomorrow. You have my word."

"And in the meantime?"

"I have no doubt Richard will improve; he always has in the past. He has known these attacks before. He is resting quietly now. Dr. Gideon said he would sleep until evening."

Sarah was taken aback by this sudden reasonableness on John's part. It was as if he had switched back to the man she had first met in Edinburgh — the John Stone of sympathy and intelligence. And she felt a rush of guilt that she had been so quick to condemn him. She should be equally fair to him and tell him all she knew. In this fresh rush of faith she thought she should mention the weird incident Richard had recited to her.

"Richard told me a strange story." She paused. "Has he ever spoken to you of ghostly visits of his mother?"

John looked shocked. "No. Never!"

"He has mentioned them to me."

"When?"

"Several times. And this morning when I went up to see him he told me that his mother visited him in the night and gave him some sweet liquid to drink."

The blond man frowned. "But that's completely fantastic!"

"I agree it is hard to accept. Yet he

seemed very clear on the details of all that took place."

"The boy was suffering from pain and fever," John explained wearily. "He was thinking of his dead mother, and that is how it came out."

"I have tried to persuade myself of that," she admitted. "But there is still a lingering doubt. This is such a strange old house, it seems anything might be possible here."

His face was sad. "Then accept that the lad was visited by the ghost of his mother," he said. "But don't try to tell me she would do anything to hurt the child she loved above all else."

She saw how right his logic was and the grievous error of thinking into which she had fallen. "You are right, of course," she said quietly.

"And as for Penelope," he continued in the same sad vein, "I loved her with all my being. I ask you to believe that."

Sarah got up, feeling it was time to leave. She said, "Thank you for being so considerate of me. Your explanations have rid my mind of a good deal of confusion. I'll be relieved to have the other doctor see Richard tomorrow."

"I promise you that I'll send for him," John Stone said quietly. "And there is one other thing. It puzzles me that you have not come to know it."

She looked at him. "And what is that?"

"I love you," he said with quiet simplicity. "I have since the first day I saw you in that courtroom."

"No," she said in a whisper. "You cannot mean it!"

He took her by the arms, his expression still grave. "Is the idea so distasteful to you? Can you not understand that a lonely man such as myself might find solace in a lovely person like you?"

She shook her head. "You have given no sign of it! We have become almost enemies. I would have written the judge to take me back to Edinburgh had I not been so concerned for Richard."

"I know you've picked up a lot of distorted ideas about me. I imagine Rodney has helped contribute to them. And perhaps my own actions — I realize some of them may be difficult to understand. But I beg of you, have faith in me and my sincere feelings for you."

She turned her head aside as he drew her closer to him. "Please!" she said. "Give me a little time. I'm not able to think clearly."

"You shall have all the time you need," he assured her, tender eyes studying her.

"And what of Abigail?" she asked. "Surely she also loves you and thinks you may marry her?"

He smiled sadly. "You have it wrong there. It is Rodney whom Abigail cares for. And he has no wish to marry anyone."

Sarah thought of the moments she had spent in Rodney's arms only last night. It was true he had offered her comfort, and his caresses had been ardent enough. But he had only suggested he might fall in love with her. There had been none of the certainty that John evidenced now that he held her in his embrace.

She said, "In the beginning I thought of you as someone special. The finest person I had ever met."

"Not quite that," he murmured. "But I will try to merit your love in my own humble way," and saying this he touched his lips to hers.

His kiss was not as long or as ardent as the one by Rodney, but somehow she felt it much more convincing. When they parted she stared up at the blond man with shining eyes, certain that he loved her.

He still held her by the arms, a rare smile on his handsome face. "It is possible I may try your patience again. There are some important matters to be taken care of before we can settle down in happiness."

"First let us be sure that Richard has proper care," she said.

He nodded. "I promise that."

There was a parting kiss, and then she went upstairs to her own room. She was filled with a new mood of content and joy, but unhappily it was not to last long. Perhaps the dreary day was to blame, along with her worry about Richard deep in the drugged slumber induced by Dr. Gideon's tincture of opium; but chiefly it was the nagging doubts of the many unanswered questions that plagued her.

John had caught her completely off guard with his declaration of love for her. His willingness to at last call in another doctor had also come as a startling surprise in view of his previous stubborn stand. These things had temporarily blocked her mind to the many troubling, even terrifying, questions that remained to be answered.

He had asked for her faith in him, and she desperately longed to be able to offer that steadfast belief. But she knew in her heart that she couldn't. Not yet. John had been condemning in his mention of Rodney, and she could not agree with him in that. Nor had he offered any reasonable explanation for the many macabre happenings.

She sat by the window of her room for a long time, pondering these things. She wondered if Rodney had returned. She had seen him leave in a rage early in the morning, and he had not put in an appearance since. Surely it would be helpful to talk to him.

A sound from the hallway interrupted her thoughts, and she got up and moved toward her door. She was sure she heard familiar footsteps along the corridor, John's footsteps. And thinking she might have a word with him, she opened the door to stare out into the gloomy corridor. But he had passed by, and she caught only a glimpse of him as he mounted the stairs to the attic.

A bit disappointed, she shut the door and went back to sit by the window. The grounds looked especially bleak in this wet weather, and she wondered what John might be doing upstairs. No doubt delving into some of those crates that were still nailed up. He was apparently making a complete list of all the items that had been shipped to him.

And then she was startled to hear the familiar slam of the door upstairs, the sound that had awakened her before during the night. She looked up at the ceiling and she heard quick footsteps, then the rumble of John's voice raised in anger. No words came through clearly, but there was no mistaking his tone.

As if to climax it all, she heard a sharp feminine cry of anguish, and then loud weeping. Sarah got to her feet with a shocked expression on her pretty face and strained to hear more of what was going on. But all was silent.

Filled with a consuming curiosity she left her room for the darkness of the corridor and slowly made her way toward the attic steps. The steps that John Stone had warned her not to use!

She was certain she could hear him now, giving low, urgent instructions to someone. And along with it there was a string of protests and whimpering in a female voice. The two were having a savage argument. There could be no doubt of that. She was anxious to continue eavesdropping, but feared the consequences should John come down and see her there.

Fright making her lovely face pale, she glanced about for a spot of refuge and saw a suitably recessed doorway. She thought if she crouched close to it, the darkness would hide her from anyone who might come by. Hastily she made a furtive passage across the corridor and took her position, still trying to hear what was going on in the attic.

The door closed once again, and as she pressed back in the shadows she thought she heard soft footsteps along the corridor above. Her heart pounded frantically as she heard the footsteps descending the steep stairs of the attic. Next they would be coming along the hallway past her. But she didn't dare venture to peer out to get an advance view of who it might be. Instead she remained completely motionless, scarcely daring to breathe as she waited.

The figure that passed her was Abigail, and although she had only a brief glimpse of the girl's lovely face, she could see that it was tear-stained. Abigail hurried on, and a moment later she heard the door close on her room a distance away.

Sarah waited for several minutes longer, thinking John might follow the weeping girl down. But there was no sound of him. Finally she left her hiding place and hurried back to her own room, where she slid the bolt and threw herself on the bed, her eyes brimming with tears.

So that was it! John Stone had deliberately led her on and lied to her about his love for her when all the time he and Abigail were playing their murderous game. Naturally Abigail had resented his attentions to her and had no doubt taken him to task about it. That would explain the tense quarrel that had gone on above and Abigail's appearing in tears.

The brief span of happiness she'd known fled before this shocking revelation. Now she must somehow find her way out of this maze of evil on her own. But not completely alone, for there was Rod to count on. But she could not look to John Stone for help or sincerity. Whatever his reasons, he was deeply involved in some diabolical scheme.

As she gradually recovered from the first shock of her discovery she began to see that she must be extremely wary. She must also play a part, so as not to put John and Abigail on their guard. It would seem that she would have to pretend that she'd accepted John Stone's declaration of love as sincere, however hateful it might be now that she knew the truth. And she must hope that he would at least live up to his promise to summon the other doctor for Richard.

She got up from the bed to change for dinner just as there came a soft knock at her door.

9

She approached the door cautiously. "Yes?"

From the other side a familiar voice said, "It's Rod. Could I have a minute with you?"

She was relieved, even pleased, to hear him. And without giving a thought to the possible impropriety of it, she opened the door quickly and let him in. He was wearing a cloak over his clothes and a battered black felt hat, and looked for all the world the romantic picture of a poet.

When she had closed the door, he said, "I've just come back from the village. The rain is stopping. What did the doctor say?"

Sarah smelled whisky on Rodney's breath, saw his flushed cheeks, and knew he had been drinking heavily. She said, "He came only a little while after you left. He gave Richard some tincture of opium and said he would sleep for a time and come out of his spell."

"The usual remedy," Rodney grumbled. "Not good enough."

"I asked Dr. Gideon if the boy hadn't been poisoned, and he suggested there might be something wrong with the estate's drinking water."

"Aye," the poet said sagely. "My guess is there's more awry than just the water."

"One other thing," she said. "John has promised that he will have Dr. MacGregor see the boy tomorrow."

The dark-haired man lifted his eyebrows. "Now that's a new tack for him."

"He came around to it very easily. I was surprised."

Rodney nodded. "As well you might be. I'll believe it when I see it. I'm inclined to look on it as one of his sly tricks."

"If it is, we'll soon know."

"I wouldn't want to stand on one foot waiting for Dr. MacGregor to show up," Rodney said disgustedly. "I'll wager he's never been sent for."

She was beginning to wonder about it as well. Especially in the light of John's other deceits. But she wasn't able to divulge the full story to Rodney. She could not do that without telling him of John's spurious declaration of love for her, and that would be too humiliating. Suddenly aware of the position she had placed herself in by allowing Rodney in her room, she decided he must go at once.

"I shouldn't have let you come in here," she said. "They'll be watching us more closely than ever if they catch you visiting me."

"I need more time to talk," Rodney insisted. "There are things I have thought out I couldn't tell you yesterday. About up there!" He rolled his eyes to indicate the attic. "Up there where he has all his dark sorcery from Egypt! It's brought us a curse as sure as there's heather on the heath!"

"Please, you must go!" she urged.

"Meet me after dinner then."

"Where?"

"Down by the bench where we talked last night?"

She hesitated. "It may still be raining, and anyway the grass will be wet."

"Let's have no excuses," Rodney said. "What I have to tell you is important."

"I think we were seen last night," she told him. "I won't come until dusk. That way we run less risk of being spied on."

"Have it as you wish," Rodney said, his hand on the doorknob. "I'll be there waiting for you."

She managed to urge the tipsy poet on his way, and worried that even as things stood someone might have seen him entering and leaving her room. It was getting late, and she hurried to dress for dinner. It was not a meal she looked forward to. She couldn't help wondering how John and the demure Abigail would act.

If she had anticipated a change in the two she was in for a disappointment. They behaved exactly as before. Possibly Abigail was a fraction more subdued and talked even less than usual, but John was as stern and cold as on the other evenings. He unbent only now and then when he gave her an approving glance.

For her part she was desperately nervous, feeling that the eyes of all the others at the table were appraising her. And her position was not made more comfortable by Rodney's drunken jests. He kept twitting his half brother and making vague references to those who bound themselves over to witchcraft and sorcery.

With a smile her way, Rodney leaned close and said, "The devil himself is a friend of all us Scots. We call him Auld Nick and Auld Clootie, and we take him to our hearts! We don't need witchcraft from the Nile!"

Sarah knew he was trying to annoy John and was careful not to offer him too much encouragement. "I know nothing of

Scottish lore," she said.

Rodney chuckled drunkenly. "It was the devil who played the pipes at the witches' dance in Kirk Alloway. Warlocks and witches in a dance!"

John frowned at him from the head of the table. "You seem strangely preoccupied with the devil and such tonight."

Rodney leered at him. "Just because I don't spend hours of my days and nights brooding over the bodies of heathen dead in the attic and experimenting with their secret potions and spells doesn't mean I know nothing of the mystic!"

"I'm sure it doesn't," John said with anger, his handsome face outlined by the glow of the candles on the table.

Rodney nodded slyly. "I may even have a surprise or two in store for those that set such store by the same." He turned to Sarah. "All the village is talking about the hauntings of Priscilla Kirk of late. And how, as a Scottish wraith, she resents John's Egyptian devils!"

"There has been enough loose talk at the table," John declared sternly. "I suggest you reserve it for the taverns, where you've obviously spent all day."

Rodney rose from the table with drunken gravity, and pointing an accusing finger at his brother, said, "There are discoveries a man cannot live with without resorting to the drink!" And having delivered himself of this, he straightened up carefully and made his way from the dining room, swaying only a little.

Consternation showed on John's face in the wake of his brother's departure. "I have never heard him talk like that before."

Abigail gave him a reproving glance. "It was not Rodney talking; it was the drink."

"Even so, he took liberties for which I'll not easily forgive him," John said. "And when he is sober tomorrow I'll tell him so."

The meal ended on a sour note. And Abigail, continuing her strangely subdued behavior, left the room. John escorted Sarah out and seemed in a talkative mood.

"Perhaps we ought to look in on Richard," he suggested. "I have asked Mrs. Fergus to stay with him."

"I would like to see how he is," Sarah agreed at once. "Did you get a message off to Dr. MacGregor?"

"I sent one of the stable lads," John said absently. But there was a singular lack of conviction in his tone. She was afraid that Rodney was right. And she wondered how much of his drunkenness at the table was real and how much feigned so that he could give rein to his sharp tongue and torment John. She would know when she met with him later on.

Richard was sitting up in bed when they entered his room. His small face took on a smile of pleasure on seeing Sarah, and he said, "I've been hoping you'd come."

Sarah went over and touched her lips to his forehead and was shocked that he was still so feverish. She thought he looked wan and pinched, but at least he didn't seem to be in any pain.

She said, "I can see you're feeling better."

"Yes," he nodded solemnly. "I have not had any pains in my tummy, and Mrs. Fergus gave me some broth just now."

Sarah smiled at the old crone who stood like a grim sentinel on the other side of the bed. "I'm sure Mrs. Fergus will bring you lots of good things to eat."

Richard appealed to his father. "Will I be able to go out tomorrow if it is fine?"

"We'll see when tomorrow comes," his father hedged. "First you must eat a little and try to get back some strength." And to Mrs. Fergus, he said, "You can give him his second dose of medicine directly, so he'll settle down to a good night's sleep."

The old woman nodded.

Sarah was not enthusiastic about Richard's care being in the hands of the slightly mad Mrs. Fergus, and when they had left the sick room she told John as much. "Do you consider Mrs. Fergus fit to take care of the boy?"

He showed surprise. "She's very fond of him."

"Nevertheless, she isn't completely reliable," Sarah said, worried. "And an overdose of that tincture of opium could be fatal."

John shrugged. "I gave her careful instructions. I'm sure she knows the exact dosage."

"I'll be glad when Dr. MacGregor sees Richard," she said with a sigh. "I think there must be better medicine for him than what Dr. Gideon prescribed."

"I wonder," John said, as they went downstairs. "Personally I have great confidence in the old man."

They talked for a few minutes in the hallway, but there was none of the warmth between them that had existed for those few minutes in his study that morning. Sarah was more than ever convinced that John had meant none of the things he had said, and she was anxious to make plans with Rodney as to how they might get Dr. MacGregor to come and see Richard.

John murmured that he had some work to do in his study, and they parted. She went upstairs to get her cloak and put on her heavy shoes. The rain had ended, but in its wake there had come a heavy fog that now wreathed the grounds in a ghostly shroud. In a way she was grateful for it, as it would serve to give her rendezvous with Rodney even more privacy.

She made her way downstairs without meeting anyone and left the house quickly, being careful to close the door gently. It was still not completely dark, but the fog added to the murkiness of the late evening. She walked swiftly until she felt the fog curtained her, shutting her off from the house. Then she made her way to the marble bench where she had talked with Rodney the night before.

He was not there.

She stood frowning, wondering what could be delaying him. And she began to fear that his behavior at the table had not been feigned but only too real. Possibly Rodney had gone to his room and fallen into a deep drunken slumber. By the time he woke up and remembered he'd promised to meet her, it might well be the middle of the night.

On the slim chance that he might have

encountered some minor delay, she waited. But as the minutes passed and he still did not come, she became certain he had failed her. It was an unhappy situation, but one she should have been prepared for in dealing with Rodney.

The light was growing dim and the fog swirled about the hedges even thicker than before. It gave the night an especially eerie atmosphere, she thought, and she shivered and pulled her cloak about her tighter. Thoroughly let down, she decided there was no point in waiting for the errant Rodney any longer. Within minutes it would be completely dark, and she had no wish to be alone in this deserted section of the grounds.

With a sigh she turned and started to re-trace her steps. She had gone only a few yards when she became aware that some-one was following her. She quickened her pace, and the speed of the footsteps behind her also increased. She turned to glance apprehensively over her shoulder and saw a weird wraithlike figure, cloaked completely in black, almost upon her.

She gave a cry of fear and began to run. And from behind there came a maniacal cackle of laughter. Sarah stumbled forward across the fog-shrouded wet grass, and it was not until one of the plaster figures loomed up before her that she realized, with horror, that she'd become confused and had been running in the wrong direction.

Panting she fell against the plaster figure, only to look up and see the mutilated, mocking face of Priscilla Kirk! With a groan she swayed, averting her eyes from the statue, when suddenly the dark phantom descended on her. She screamed again as she saw an upraised hand, and plunged forward in her frantic race as something ripped through her cloak, making a great rent in it. The maniacal laughter sounded again.

Her panic gave her the needed strength to race on with new energy. She thought she was going in the proper direction this time, but there was no chance of pausing to make sure. Somewhere close on her heels was the phantom creature that had caught up with her long enough to once again slash at her clothes. She pressed on, her lungs screaming with pain and struggling for breath.

When she thought she must finally stop and throw herself on the ground to scream for mercy she lifted her eyes to see the towering old mansion looming out of the fog before her tortured view. She voiced a prayer of thanks and forced herself forward until she fell up the porch steps. Grasping a post, she turned to glance behind her with terror still dilating her lovely eyes.

There was just the fog. The unknown thing that had pursued her and had slashed at her was nowhere to be seen. Darkness was at hand as she stood there, her breath still coming in great sobbing gulps. She examined her cloak and saw the great rent that stretched almost the full length of the cloak. It was a repeat of what had happened the first night, in the corridor.

Her breathing more nearly normal, she stared out into the fog once more, certain that somewhere out there lurked the wild thing that had marked her for a victim. She did not know whether it was of this earth, or the avenging ghost of Priscilla Kirk, or even some sinister dark creature released from the stone sarcophagus in the attic to prey on all those who opposed John Stone's will; but she felt that on this night she had once again come near to death!

When she entered the old mansion it was grimly silent. No one was in sight in the area of the hallway, and she made her way up the broad stairway as quickly as she could. She had a strong desire to go directly to Rodney's room and knock on his door. But she decided this wouldn't be wise. If he were really in a drunken slumber she could hardly hope to rouse him and would only attract the attention of the others. Better to go to her own room and wait until she heard from him. And bolt herself in.

She was undressed and in bed when she again heard footsteps above, along with John Stone's angry rumble and the voice of a woman. This time the exchange between the two was brief. And shortly afterward she heard light footsteps going along the corridor by her door and decided it must be Abigail going downstairs.

She found sleep elusive and lay awake trying to decide what she would do next. Because of her state of nerves she had lighted the candle on her bedside table, and its flickering flame offered her some solace. She had almost fallen asleep when she heard the sound of heavy uneven footsteps coming down the corridor.

Rising up in bed she stared at the bolted door and tried to locate the sound. The footsteps were coming nearer. Next there was a heavy pounding on her door, and she heard Rodney calling her name in a slurred voice.

She rose hastily, threw on her dressing gown, and went to the door. "It's all right," she said through the door. "I'm back safely. Please go away. I'll see you to-morrow." She guessed that he had roused from his drunken sleep, had started to worry about her, and had come to apologize in his alcoholic confusion.

"Let me in!" he persisted in his thick voice, and pounded loudly again.

"Please, Rod!" she begged.

"Have to see you!" He kept on pounding.

Desperate, she saw no alternative but to open the door and try to placate him and send him back to his room. She pictured everyone else being attracted by his commotion as it was.

She slid back the bolt and opened the door to see a thoroughly drunken Rodney swaying there. Again she entreated him, "Please go back to your own room!"

He lifted a hand, and forming his words with great difficulty, said, "Serious! Must tell you!"

There was a look in his glazed eyes that told Sarah there was something more wrong with him than mere drink.

She stepped forward to support his swaying form. "Rod! What is it?"

He struggled to focus his eyes on her and tell her something. After an agonizing moment he gasped, "The drink!" And in spite of her efforts his sturdy young body toppled to the floor.

She knelt by him crying, "Rod! Rod! What's wrong?"

So engrossed was she in her efforts to revive him that she did not hear the approach of the others. Then she glanced up with a stricken face to see John standing beside her. Abigail was close behind him, and in the rear stood a sour-visaged Mrs. Fergus.

Sarah said, "I don't know what's happened to him."

John's face was stern. "I have a good idea."

"I know what you're thinking," she said. "But I'm certain it's more than just drink."

"I've seen him like this before," John said angrily. "I'll take him back to his room." And he bent to grab the motionless Rodney under the armpits and drag him down the corridor.

Sarah followed for a few steps. "Please be sure he's all right." And then she stopped, noticing that Abigail and the old woman were giving her curious looks.

She turned to Abigail. "I think he's ill as well as very drunk."

The girl's eyes looked as if she'd been crying. She said, "No need to concern yourself; it's an old business with him."

Sarah was shocked. "I had no idea he could be this bad."

"Because you don't know him as we do," Abigail said. "You'd best get back to bed."

"Yes." Sarah turned to go back, then hesitated, to ask over her shoulder, "Let me know if there is anything else wrong."

Abigail nodded. "Yes."

Reluctantly Sarah went back to her room and bolted the door. In spite of what the others had said, she was still of the opinion Rodney Stone wasn't merely drunk. There was something else wrong with him. She couldn't picture his neglecting to meet her, as he'd promised, then making a scene to attract the household by coming to her door in an alcoholic daze.

It was another troubling incident in a night that had included more than its share of them. She found it impossible to settle down in bed, and instead went to the window and parted the drapes to stare out into the fog. It had not lifted. She was still standing at the window when the gentle rap came at her door.

She moved a few steps toward it. "Yes?"

"It's me. John."

"Oh," she said, and advanced several steps more. "Is Rodney all right?"

"Open up," John said. "I want to explain."

Sarah felt a slight sensation of fear, and yet it seemed highly unlikely that the master of Dankhurst would attempt to harm her with everyone in the house aroused. Slowly she slid the bolt and swung the door open.

He stepped into the candle-lit room. Looking at her with concern, he asked, "Are you all right?"

"Yes. What about Rodney?"

"I've put him to bed. He should be fine in the morning, except for a bad hangover. But I intend to give him a severe talking to."

Sarah looked up at the stern face of this man who was undoubtedly leading some kind of double life. She said, "He seemed to want to tell me something."

"I was afraid he might have mauled you!"

She shook her head. "No. He didn't touch me. I tried to support him, to keep him from falling."

"I see," John said. "Let me apologize for his behavior."

"That's not necessary."

"I really feel very bad about it, Sarah," he said, lingering over her name as he said it.

"We'll just forget it," she said in an effort to dismiss him, feeling vaguely uneasy at the way his eyes were boring into hers. "Good night, John."

"Good night, my dear," he said, and with an easy natural gesture he took her quickly in his arms for a brief kiss. With a parting nod he went out and closed the door.

She stood staring after him, the touch of his lips still fresh on hers, and wondered just what sort of man she might be dealing with. To what lengths would John go to carry through his dark plans?

The fog did not lift, and the next morning was almost as dark and gray as it had been on the preceding night. When Sarah went down to breakfast she had the feeling that a strange new brooding tension had settled over the old mansion.

She sat down to breakfast alone, and a dour Mrs. Fergus served her wordlessly. Sarah put several questions to her, but the crone appeared to have decided to go about her business without talking at all.

Sarah was anxious to hear news of Rodney, and so she was glad when Abigail came into the dining room to stand by the head of the table. She looked up at Abigail. "How is Rodney this morning?"

"He has not come down," the girl said. "He is very ill."

Sarah put down her cup. "I knew it! I knew it last night!"

Abigail Durmot's face was unusually pale. "He is in a coma," she said. "And he has been sick to his stomach a great deal."

Sarah got up. "Has a doctor been called?"

"I don't know," the girl said. "John is with him now. I expect he'll take care of things."

"But John has so little sympathy for him!" Sarah protested.

"I'm sure he'll be different now he knows Rodney is really ill."

Sarah swept past her. "I'm going upstairs to see how he is myself."

Hurrying from the dining room she started upstairs. In her mind a terrifying thought was forming. She was beginning to think Rod's illness was no natural one. That he was merely the latest victim of the diabolical events that appeared certain to ensnare them all. A feeling of entrapment was taking hold of her. Without Rodney to turn to she was indeed alone!

She did not get to his room because she met John on the second landing. The tall blond man looked thoroughly shaken.

"I want to see him," she said.

"Not now. He's in a bad state."

"I don't care!"

John shook his head. "He'll not be able to recognize you. He's slipped into complete unconsciousness."

"What have you done for him?" she demanded. "Are you content to let him die without treatment?"

"A doctor is on his way."

She was still loath to accept this. "Are you certain?"

"You will remember I sent for Dr. Mac-Gregor yesterday," he reminded her.

Sarah was skeptical. "But will he really come?"

John showed astonishment. "What makes you think otherwise?"

She had no choice but frankness. "Because I felt you made up the story about calling him in to see Richard. I had the idea you were merely humoring me."

He stared at her in silence a moment. "It seems you have some rather strange opinions about me."

She was about to ask his permission again to see Rodney, and insist on going to the sick man's room with or without his approval, when she heard Abigail call up

from the bottom hall: "John! Dr. Mac-
Gregor is just coming into the driveway!"

He leaned over the bannister. "I'll be
right there." Then he gave Sarah a bitter
smile. "Do you need any more convincing?" And quickly started down the
stairs.

Sarah stood there, wordless. John had astonished her in this, at least. But then he
was always offering her surprises. And he
had been very ready to call in Dr.
MacGregor yesterday — so ready, that she
had suspected his motives, and still did.
However, it was no time to protest over
good fortune. Dr. MacGregor was on hand
and available to give emergency attention
to Rodney, as well as to look after the child
he had come to see.

She remained on the landing until John
returned with the doctor. Dr. MacGregor
was a severe, thin man with a small black
beard and mustache. He gave her a
brusque nod as John introduced them, and
then asked to be taken to Rodney first.

Sarah waited outside Rodney's room
while they remained inside. She paced
restlessly, anxious to hear the doctor's
opinion. After a moment she was joined by
Abigail, who had come up the stairs very
quietly.

In a low voice she asked Sarah, "Any word yet?"

"They haven't come out."

There was a period of waiting again. They both stood there without making any attempt at conversation. Then the door opened, and the two men came out, Dr. MacGregor first.

Sarah went up to him. "Can you do something for him?" she asked.

The prim bearded doctor gave her a strange look. "I fear it is now a problem of the undertaker's," he said. "Rodney Stone is dead."

10

Sarah gave a small moan. "Oh, no!"

Dr. MacGregor eyed her condescendingly. "I am not in the habit of making jests about such things, Miss Bennett." And then in a businesslike fashion, he asked, "Where will I find the boy?"

Abigail, who had begun to weep, touched a handkerchief to her eyes and volunteered, "I'll take you to him."

The two went off down the hallway leaving Sarah alone with John. She felt as if she might faint. Then the blond man's arm went around her gently to support her.

"Come now," he said. "You mustn't take on so."

She shut her eyes. "I tried to tell you. I knew he was desperately ill last night. If you'd gotten a doctor then you might have saved his life."

"I much doubt that."

"Even though he was dying he made his way to my door," she said in a small voice.

"He had something he wanted to tell me."

"What makes you so certain?" There was an edge in John's voice.

"He told me just before he collapsed."

"You shouldn't make too much of that; his mind was surely wandering."

"I don't think so."

"Let's not argue about it now," John said gently. "I'll take you downstairs and get you some brandy. You need something strong to sustain you."

She glanced toward the door. "I'd like to see him. Just for a moment."

He restrained her. "Not as he is now. Later."

She allowed him to lead her down to the first floor and into his study. He produced a bottle of brandy and poured some for her and for himself. Pressing the brandy on her he said, "Sip it. It will make you feel better."

The potent liquor burned her mouth and throat, but it did revive her somewhat. She looked up at John standing before his desk.

"What did the doctor say he died of?"

"He wasn't completely certain. I believe he intends to look further into it. Perhaps perform an autopsy."

She looked away with a pained expression. "I can't bear to think of it! Rodney was such a vital person! So generous and kind! It's hard to believe he's up there, dead."

"I confess it is a blow to me," he said, studying his glass. "Even though we were only half brothers, we were very close."

"I still can't understand it," she went on. "He seemed well enough at dinner."

"But drunken, if you will remember," John said.

"Tipsy, but not ill or completely intoxicated," she protested.

"He has long been a drinker. I've been expecting something of the sort to happen. And I warned him many times."

"You think he died from the drink alone?"

"What else?"

"Did the doctor seem to agree?" she asked.

John shrugged. "We did not take time to go into it."

She took another sip from her glass. "I feel I have lost a dear friend."

The blond man showed surprise. "Come, now, he can't have been that important to you. You've known him only a short time."

"Long enough to have a high regard for him."

John Stone downed his brandy and gave her a shrewd look. "Much more of that talk and you'll have me jealous."

She glanced at him derisively. "Jealous of a dead man?"

"He was trying to get into your room," he reminded her in a cool voice. "And as I recall, you did have a rendezvous the other night."

"To discuss the illness of your son."

"Your concern for the boy touches me," he said. "But as you see I am not stinting him in the matter of medical care."

Sarah met his cold glance. "I doubt if you'd have called Dr. MacGregor had not both Rodney and I taunted you into taking the step."

He sighed and looked down. "Perhaps you are right. At any rate, I do not want to argue about it. Poor Rod is dead, and no one will miss him more than myself."

Again she had the feeling that he had quickly changed his tone as an actor would change to a different part. It was as if he had decided to hide his true feelings behind a mask, and that from now on he would be playing a scene devised to win her sympathy.

"We can only hope the doctor will be more successful with Richard," she said.

"I'm certain he will," John said. "Although I have no quarrel with the treatment Dr. Gideon gave the child."

"I imagine Dr. MacGregor will be a trifle more perceptive."

"No doubt," he agreed. "This business will be hard on Abigail as well. She had more love for Rodney than she let others see."

"That was not his story."

"Rod was wary of all girls," John said with a sad smile. "But Abigail was closest to his heart."

Sarah knew this to be untrue and wondered why John would lie about it. Did he really believe he was deceiving her in doing so? If that was his hope he was badly mistaken, for she was on to the game between him and Abigail. She had heard their arguments in the attic too often.

Now there was the sound of voices in the hallway as Dr. MacGregor and Abigail drew close. They were talking in subdued tones, and when they came into the study she could tell they had been having a serious discussion.

John spoke up: "Well, Doctor, what about the lad?"

"He is in no danger," Dr. MacGregor said.

"That is good news," John said. "Have you been able to determine his illness and what may be the remedy?"

The doctor frowned. "I'll hazard a guess," he said. "I think the lad suffered an attack of food poisoning."

Sarah had to restrain herself from making a triumphant comment. She only wished Rodney were there to hear their suspicions confirmed. Now he would never know.

John registered surprise. "He has had similar spells before. Would you say he suffered food poisoning on all the other occasions?"

"I could not say that," Dr. MacGregor said. "But I can tell you he shows all the symptoms of that condition now."

John sighed. "Dr. Gideon hinted at something of the kind and wondered whether our water supply might be tainted."

"It is a possibility," the doctor agreed. "But then I would expect other members of the household to show similar symptoms of illness, and it seems none have."

"None except my half brother."

"I have not decided yet what caused his death," Dr. MacGregor said. "I will be able to offer an opinion after I have made a more thorough examination."

"This is a sad business. What do you prescribe for my son?"

"I will leave some powders," the doctor said. "And we will see if he has any recurrence. He should be up and about by tomorrow. Youngsters recover quickly from a condition like this, if it's not too serious."

"That is indeed good news." John smiled.

The bearded man gave him a sharp glance. "You will forgive my asking, but do you have any arsenic in the house?"

Sarah noted John's sudden frown and the glance he exchanged with a pale Abigail. The blond man said uneasily, "I don't know that we do and then I don't know that we don't. I have servants here. The gardener might have some for the rose garden. We haven't been bothering much with the rest of the grounds. Why do you ask?"

"It is a common poison that produces illness not unlike that suffered by your son, if administered in small amounts," the doctor said. "It occurred to me that someone might be handling it carelessly, and that the boy accidentally got some."

"I hardly think it possible," John protested.

"You'd be surprised how often it happens," Dr. MacGregor said. "And with parents who pride themselves on taking good care of their children."

"I will surely look into the matter," John said nervously. "It's upsetting just to think about."

"The boy is safe now, so you needn't worry," Dr. MacGregor said. "But I felt I should make mention of it. A warning might prevent its happening again."

"Yes indeed, Doctor." John gave Sarah a nervous glance. "This has been upsetting to us all. Especially to Miss Bennett, who is new to our household."

Sarah felt all the interest in the room focus on her, and again she decided that it was no accident. She was sure John had quickly brought up her name to change the subject. He had done it with a reason.

The severe bearded face of Dr. Mac-Gregor showed new interest. His sharp eyes studied her. "Bennett," he said. . . . "Miss Sarah Bennett. The name has a familiar ring. To be sure! Were you not the young woman in the Gordon case?"

Why should she deny it? Quietly she said, "Yes."

"Well!" the doctor stared at her. "I followed the case with great interest. There was certain medical evidence that had special appeal for me. As I recall it, the verdict was 'not proven.' Am I correct?"

She nodded. "That is so."

"Well, the evidence was very confusing, and I suppose the jury felt that was as far as they could venture. At any rate, it gave you your freedom."

"Yes," she said, "I am free."

"The attorney for the defense was excellent in his summing up. I read the full account of the trial in the Edinburgh paper. And the judge struck me as being on your side."

"He was very kind to me," she agreed.

The bearded man cleared his throat. "I'm afraid then I have a rather sad bit of news for you. I doubt if you've heard it, for it happened so recently. But I was in Edinburgh yesterday and picked up the information. The judge who presided over your trial took a stroke a few days ago and is now dead and buried."

John looked startled, and Sarah rose in shock. "Oh, no!"

Dr. MacGregor nodded sagely. "I am sorry to bring you the news. But then he was an old man. One must look for these things." And turning to John, he said, "I marvel our good Dr. Gideon keeps on. He is a wonder!"

"Indeed," John agreed. "You will be kind enough to notify the undertaker about my brother when you return to Rawlwyn."

"I will do that, surely," Dr. MacGregor said, and started to leave. At the door he turned and asked, "Your late wife — she died from some sort of wasting disease, did she not?"

John nodded. "Yes. I fear my son inherited his delicate constitution from her."

The doctor pursed his lips. "That is often the case, though I do not say it has to be true where your son is concerned. Dr. Gideon treated your wife, did he not?"

John nodded. "That is so." And again he glanced at Abigail, who looked as if she might faint.

Dr. MacGregor fixed him with those shrewd eyes once more. "What did Dr. Gideon decide caused your wife's death?"

"I believe the certificate said heart failure," John said.

The doctor nodded. "Interesting. I must talk with Dr. Gideon about that. Find out what he thinks brought about the heart failure. It could prove valuable to me in treating the boy. Such histories are always most helpful." He bowed to Abigail and Sarah. "Goodby, ladies. I trust my next visit will not have such sad associations." And he left, with John following him to his carriage.

Abigail said nothing for a moment. Then

she turned to Sarah with a strange look. "He recognized you," she said.

"Yes. John made sure of that."

Abigail crimsoned. "I'm sure that was not his intention."

"His intentions are more and more a puzzle to me," Sarah told her evenly.

"You must not be too hard on him," Abigail protested. "He is in a state of shock because of Rodney's death."

Sarah shook her head. "There was not that much love between them."

"You don't truly know," Abigail said with a touch of anger. "You came here as a stranger."

John Stone returned, looking pale and actually ill. He stood just inside the doorway and told Abigail, "I wish you'd go upstairs and assist Mrs. Fergus. It will only be a short time until the undertaker arrives."

Abigail hesitated, showing she would have preferred not to go, but then meekly bowed her head. "Yes," she said, and went out.

John closed the door after her, and when he and Sarah were alone he came over with a strained look on his face, and taking her by the arms, said, "Well, you would have me call in Dr. MacGregor, and now you see what has come of it!"

She stared at him in alarm. "What do you mean?"

"He recognized you. He knows you were the accused in the Gordon poisoning case."

"Why should I mind?"

"You don't understand!" he said in a strained voice. "You have no idea how small-minded these village people can be, including Dr. MacGregor. He will gossip about it on all his calls, make a local sensation of it."

"Along with his mention that he thinks Richard was poisoned?" she asked pointedly.

"It started him thinking along those lines," he said with a touch of anger. "Then he dug up that old business about my wife's death! And heaven only knows what he'll say brought about poor Rodney's end!"

"If your conscience is clear you have nothing to fear," she told him.

His grip on her arms tightened. "That is what you say. But it is far from the truth. In these places men go to the gallows on mere suspicion!"

"My experience with Scottish justice was not so unhappy."

"You were lucky," he told her. "And you can be sure Dr. MacGregor thinks so. He has you down as guilty in his mind. Don't doubt that."

She tried to free herself from him. "I'm tired, John. I'd like to go to my room."

"In a moment," he said, looking into her eyes. "Except for Richard, I have only you now. Promise me you won't desert me."

She shook her head. "This is no time for such talk."

"I need your assurance," he pleaded.

"We will decide later," she said in a small even voice.

Apparently he saw she was resolute, for he changed his tone. "You are right," he said. "I shouldn't be so impatient." And he drew her close for a moment and kissed her forehead. Then he led her to the door and opened it. "Soon all this nightmare will be at an end," he promised.

She had no faith in his words. She made her way up to her own room in a daze. And when she closed the door and slid the bolt she fell upon the bed and began to weep in grief and despair.

It was some time before she ended her sobbing, and it left her exhausted and filled with a frightening emptiness. There was no one to turn to now! No one! Even the judge was dead. And soon the undertaker's cart would be coming to take poor

Rodney's cold body. How long would she survive in this house of terror?

She didn't know what kind of game John was playing now. But in spite of his protests, she was sure he had meant Dr. MacGregor to recognize her. She felt helplessly inadequate to cope with the blond man and his accomplice. The memory of those terrible moments in the fog last night still haunted her.

When her capacity for grief was exhausted she began to think of the child. And after she had carefully washed her face and powdered it to hide the ravages of her tears she made her way to Richard's room.

The little boy was sitting up in bed in the darkened room with a toy soldier in his hand. There were a small company of them spread out on the coverlet. He looked much better and greeted her with a smile.

He showed her the lead soldier proudly and announced, "He's just taken the queen's shilling and he's being sent to India with the rest of the soldiers."

"Well," she said. "He's going to have a long voyage."

Richard gave her a questioning look. "Is it true about Uncle Rodney?"

"What?" she hesitated to answer him fully.

"Mrs. Fergus says the devil came and got him and took him away. I guess he'll be going on a long voyage. Even farther than India." He looked at her pensively. "Will the devil let him come back?"

She sat on his bed, and with a sad smile told him, "I don't think Mrs. Fergus has the facts completely right. The truth is that Rodney has gone to join your mother. I'm sure they'll be having a happy reunion."

The boy's eyes widened. "Oh! You mean he's dead?"

"Yes."

"But he wasn't sick like my mummy."

"No," she said. "He died very suddenly. It came as a terrible shock to everyone. So you must try to understand."

"I will ask Mummy about him when she comes in the night," the boy said fondling a toy soldier.

The chilling fear stabbed her again. "Richard," she said, "you're just saying that, aren't you? I mean, you like to make up a pretty story about your mummy visiting you. And there's really nothing very wrong in that if it gives you any comfort. But I want you to tell me the truth. She doesn't really come in here to see you in the middle of the night, does she?"

He stared at her wide-eyed for a moment. Then very solemnly he said, "I wouldn't lie to you, Sarah. She has come, three or four times, and she'll come again. She said she would."

"I see," she said in a near whisper. And then, looking at him earnestly, she added, "There is just one thing I want you to promise me."

His little face showed interest. "What?"

"If your mummy comes again, and if she offers you anything to drink or eat, tell her you don't want it."

"But she would be cross with me."

"I don't think so. Not if she loves you. And if she makes you take it, you can pretend to drink or eat whatever it is, and either spill it, or hide it in your bed. Will you promise me that?"

"Why, Sarah?" His blue eyes were puzzled.

How could she explain? It would be useless to try and tell him the truth. And then she searched wildly for something he would understand. "Well," she said at last, "it's because the food she brings you is from another land — the land where she lives now. And it's a kind of magic food that is good for her but doesn't agree with you. If you eat it or drink any of that sweet drink, you may be sick again like you were yesterday."

"It's a magic food," he said, his eyes wide with wonder.

"Yes. And not good for little boys. Remember that."

"I will," he promised.

"Good," she said. And not wanting to burden his little mind with any more of this kind of talk she turned the attention to his toy army. "Now tell me more about your soldiers and what they are going to do."

"I'll tell you about their regiment," he said with small-boy importance, and began to give her an account of his particular branch of the red-coated army. She listened, not really hearing what he was saying.

I've tried, she told herself; at least I've tried!

The undertaker returned with Rodney's body in a rich oak casket the next morning, and it was set up in state in the living room under the portrait of old Stephen Dank.

The undertaker was a wizened little man with a sad smile who looked as if he had been preserved with his own embalming fluid. When the casket had been set up and

John, Abigail, and Sarah, along with Mrs. Fergus and the other servants, had been assembled, the little man removed the cover to reveal Rodney's remains.

"A beautiful corpse," he said proudly.

And it was true. Rodney looked as handsome in death as he ever had in life. Any trace of those turbulent final hours had been erased from his countenance by the magic of the little undertaker. The servants passed by to pay their respects, and then John and the two women were left alone in the big room.

John sighed. "We will have some busy days. Half the county will be coming to pay their respects."

He was right. Sarah was astonished at the number of people who visited the estate to say goodby to Rodney Stone. John and Abigail took turns at greeting the mourners, and Sarah spent most of her time upstairs with little Richard. The child was feeling much better, and Dr. MacGregor had called again and ordered the windows left opened and the curtains drawn back so that the room might be filled with fresh air. It was a move Sarah heartily approved of.

At night the old estate took on its most lonely aspect. When the darkness closed in

Sarah was constantly aware of Rodney's body resting in its coffin below. She still found it hard to believe he was dead. Once she asked John what the doctor had said was the cause of death, and John had said curtly that he hadn't been told.

On the final night before the burial she decided she would venture down alone and pay a final tribute to Rodney, who had truly been her friend. She waited until she was certain all the others had gone to bed. Then taking along a lighted candle, she quietly made her way down the stairs. The old mansion had never seemed so eerie.

Only her determination to show her respect for Rodney kept her to her decision. Twice on the way down she heard strange sounds on the steps behind her. She paused to turn around and stare into the darkness. But she saw nothing and put it down to nerves.

At the bottom of the stairs the vaulted ceiling of the lower hallway made the glow from her candle seem a poor thing. She stood there in the cool gloom and uneasy silence of the great house, summoning the courage to go in and take up her short vigil by the casket.

Moving slowly toward the double doors she was suddenly frozen by a muffled sound from the living room. It came from the area where Rodney's casket was, and there was no mistaking the sound of feminine weeping. She had heard the same weeping before from the attic on other occasions, and she didn't need to venture farther into the room to know it was Abigail who must be sobbing beside the body of Rodney.

Sarah had an impulse to go into the room and offer sympathy to the stricken girl. Then she realized that it might be sympathy that wasn't wanted, sympathy that would be but a mockery! Because Abigail Durmot might have a reason of conscience for weeping over the dead Rodney. John and Abigail might well have conspired to bring about Rodney's death, just as they had with Penelope. For she believed the two had gotten her out of the way and had plotted against Richard. Surely it had been Abigail who had entered his room, posing as his dead mother, and offered him a poisoned drink.

Troubled by these thoughts, she decided the best thing she could do was to go quietly back to her own room. She was sure Rodney would understand and approve. Whatever the reason for Abigail's show of grief, Sarah had no right to intrude on it.

She made her way up the dark stairs, still hearing the bitter sobs in her mind, and wondering what the next turn of events would be.

The morning of the funeral brought sunshine and warm weather again. It was as bright as one of Rodney's smiles, she thought sadly, as she put on her good black dress for the occasion. She and Richard would go to the kirk in Rawlwyn in the same carriage, and she would take the boy to the small cemetery beside the church where Rodney was being buried in the family lot.

There was a stir in the house when she went downstairs. She joined Abigail in the dining room, but neither of them took anything other than a slice of toast and some tea. The signs of weeping were plain on the attractive girl's face, and she looked as if she'd had little or no sleep.

"When will we be leaving?" Sarah asked her.

Abigail kept her eyes on the table, to avoid looking directly at Sarah. "The plan is to leave at ten."

"Then it will not be too long," Sarah said. "I must go up and get the boy ready. What a beautiful day."

"Rod's kind of day," Abigail said quietly as she got up from the table.

She and Sarah went out into the hallway, where they could hear John and the undertaker having a brisk discussion in the living room. Sarah thought she detected a note of anger in John's voice.

Abigail showed nervousness, and led the way to the double doors and the two men who were standing just inside. Sarah saw they were staring at something on the wall.

"I thought I should draw your attention to it, sir," the undertaker said in a troubled voice.

"You did right," John said. "It must be taken down before anyone else arrives."

Sarah took a step inside to see what they were discussing, and saw it was the portrait of Justine, the portrait with the slash that Abigail had told her was reputedly made by the ghostly hand of Priscilla Kirk. The portrait was still there — what was left of it — for now someone had wildly slashed it in every direction until there was nothing of the pretty face remaining!

11

The funeral service for Rod was held in the tiny kirk of Rawlwyn, and the crowd over-flowed the rural church. Sarah and little Richard were seated behind the other mourners, and she had a good view of John Stone's handsome face all during the service. The black-robed pastor spent an inordinately long time heralding the late poet's virtues, and she could see John frown several times. When the cleric finished they filed from the church to the graveside in the small adjacent cemetery.

At the graveside Abigail Durmot wept aloud, and John put an arm around the girl to comfort her. Richard gave Sarah a questioning look, and she reassured him by squeezing his small hand. She purposely had taken a position with him a little distance from the graveside. Mrs. Fergus was there, her dour face looking more grim than usual. And the severe Dr. MacGregor was prominent among those present, as was old Dr. Gideon, leaning on a thick walking stick and wearing a sad, vexed expression on his wrinkled face.

Despite her feeling of sadness at this final moment of parting from the likable Rodney, Sarah found her mind wandering to another matter and trying to decide its significance. She was sure the complete destruction of Justine's portrait had a meaning, but she could not guess what it might be. Whoever had slashed it so that there was no longer any real likeness, had done so for a reason. There was a message there, but she lacked the knowledge to read it.

When the undertaker had helped John take the portrait down she had heard the master of Dankhurst refer to the actions of vandals once again, but she had felt this was an unsatisfactory explanation. She could not see any outsider coming into the mansion and destroying the portrait — certainly not with Rod resting in his casket in the same room! Easier to believe in the avenging wraith of Priscilla Kirk.

With the brief service at the graveside ended, a large part of the group began to disperse. Some close friends remained to crowd about John and Abigail and offer their condolences. Because Sarah and Richard were a distance away they avoided this. She felt it was preferable, as she did not want the child to be exposed to more of the melancholy ritual than was necessary. She hoped they would soon be able to return to their carriage and make the journey back to Dankhurst.

Richard was uneasy. He lifted his small pale face to her and asked, "Aren't we going home now?"

"In a moment," she promised him. And looking up, she saw a figure approaching them at a snail's pace. It was the top-hatted and black-garbed Dr. Gideon, with a purposeful look on his face, coming forward.

"Ah!" he said with satisfaction as he paused before them and smiled at Richard. "I'm glad to see you up and about again, young sir."

"I'm feeling much better," Richard said meekly.

"Of course you are!" Dr. Gideon exclaimed, patting the yellow head with his free hand as he rested heavily on his cane with the other. "I knew my medicine would bring you round." He peered at Sarah with myopic eyes. "And you are his governess, I presume?"

The old man must be especially alert today, Sarah thought. At least he hadn't mixed her up with the dead Penelope as he had on two previous occasions. She smiled. "Yes, I'm Miss Bennett."

Dr. Gideon glanced back toward the grave where John and Abigail were still talking with friends. He shook his head. "A sad business. I would have given Rodney half a century more of life."

"He was stricken very suddenly," she said.

The old man frowned and regarded her with vague, troubled eyes. "That household has seen more than its share of deaths of late."

"It would seem so," Sarah said.

Dr. Gideon sighed. "I attended the late Penelope Stone, who suffered from a most mysterious malady. She would recover and then sink back into serious illness again. Dr. MacGregor questioned me about it only this morning."

Sarah was at once wary. So Dr. MacGregor had been delving into the past events at Dankhurst. She was sure he was not satisfied with what he'd heard about Penelope's illness and death, and if he had now found suspicious facts attending Rodney's demise, not to mention Richard's illness, he might be working to bring the monstrous plot she was certain existed into the open.

Tactfully she said, "Mr. Stone called Dr. MacGregor in for a consultation on Richard's condition."

The ancient face took on a withering look of scorn. "No need of it at all," he snapped. "I already had the boy well on his way to health. And MacGregor has a probing, suspicious mind that sees shadows where they do not exist."

"I do not follow you, Doctor," she said.

Dr. Gideon appeared not to hear her, he was staring off into space and scowling. "The nerve of the young upstart asking to see my notes on the case! My notes, indeed! As if I needed notes! One would think he was suggesting I didn't know what I was doing! I gave Penelope Stone the best of care! I dare anyone to prove differently!"

"But you were not able to save her," Sarah said.

The old man's eyes became more alert. "What was I saying just now?"

Sarah said, "You were talking about Richard's mother and her illness."

Dr. Gideon showed a guilty surprise. "Was I, indeed? Now how did I get started on that?" He gave Richard a smile again. "Good to see you well once more. I must hasten and say a few words to your good father before I take my leave." And with that he hobbled off.

When he was out of earshot Richard said firmly, "I think he is a silly goose!"

Sarah could have easily agreed, but out of respect for the old doctor's age she told the boy, "I think his mind is failing because he is very old. And now we'd better return to the carriage. Your father and Abigail will be ready to begin the journey home in a few minutes."

In spite of the warm, sunny day, Dankhurst seemed even more gray and solemn than usual with Rodney no longer there. As the carriage rolled up the driveway she sat close to Richard and stared at the formidable old stone mansion with a deep feeling of melancholy. She couldn't help wondering what new tragedy awaited them there.

John was rather aloof as they went into the house, and Abigail hurried upstairs to her own room without a word to anyone. Sarah had the impression they were both suffering from guilty consciences.

John turned to her, his face a pale mask, and said, "I will count on you to keep Richard occupied for the day. I have some urgent matters to attend to that will take all my time."

"Of course," she said.

"Can we go out into the garden, Father?" Richard asked.

"I suppose so," John said absently. "Just don't overdo yourself." And he went down the hall to his study.

After a light lunch she took Richard to the rose garden where she read from *Alice In Wonderland*, a favorite of his. Somehow reading the delightful tale helped lighten her mood, as well as the boy's. Afterward they took a walk, and again he pointed out the various statues to her and named them as he had before. Sarah was filled with thoughts about these long-dead folk whom old Stephen Dank had given a macabre immortality.

Hesitating before a figure Sarah would always remember, Richard said, "And this is Priscilla Kirk."

Sarah stared at the noseless face and pocked cheeks of what had once been a youthful, smiling beauty, and in a low voice repeated, "Yes. This is Priscilla Kirk."

The night was uneventful, but Sarah was awakened the next morning by vigorous hammering from the end of the corridor. She got out of bed, listened at the door, and heard the sound of male voices and persons moving about. After a moment or two she realized that they were at work making some sort of repairs.

After she had dressed and was ready to go downstairs she paused in the corridor to see what was being done. To her astonishment she saw that two of the servants were busy installing a door frame and door at the bottom of the stairs leading to the attic. She wondered what it was for.

Downstairs she met John coming from the dining room. He looked much less tense than on the previous day. He paused to observe her soberly and ask, "Are you feeling more rested this morning?"

"Yes. And you?"

He sighed. "One must go on in spite of sadness. I think you should be able to resume Richard's studies today."

"I had planned to," she said. "What is being built at the end of the corridor?"

He hesitated. "I've decided to have doors installed by the attic steps at both ends of the house. In that way I can keep them locked when I'm not around and be sure that vandals do not get up there to steal or tamper with anything."

"I see," she said quietly.

"I made the decision after the damage done to Justine's portrait the other night," he said. "It is the second such instance within a short period."

Sarah thought of the weeping Abigail in the living room on the night the portrait was ripped to bits and felt she knew who was responsible for the vandalism, even though she didn't know why. She guessed John was shutting the attic off with doors possibly to prevent Abigail from disturbing him when he was up there communing with his collection of Egyptian relics — as well as to prevent anyone else such as herself from finding out more of the dark secrets associated with them.

She merely asked, "Have you any idea who might have done the damage?"

"No," he said. But there was little conviction in his tone.

"What could the motive be? I mean, why should anyone pick the same portrait to mutilate again?"

He sighed. "I have thought about it and come to several conclusions. I cannot say for sure which may be the true one." He paused, and with a change of tone, added, "We will talk about this soon when we discuss other matters pertaining to our future."

They parted, with John still behaving as if his mind were occupied with some secret problem. She did not see Abigail at breakfast and had only fleeting glimpses of her during the day. By evening the doors were securely in place at each end of the third-floor corridor, and there were padlocks on both of them.

At dinner that night they formed a silent, unhappy group. The empty chair was a grim reminder of all that had happened. Although John had made no mention of the doctor's report concerning Rod's death, Sarah had a feeling he was worried about it. It was her belief that both he and Abigail were terrified of being found out in some evil.

As dinner neared its end John announced, "Rodney's affairs are in as mixed-up a state as you would expect. I have spent all day on them, and it will mean working through the evening to get his papers in any sort of order. I will have to visit Edinburgh tomorrow and talk to his lawyer there."

Abigail raised her eyes and there was apprehension in them. "Must you leave at this time?"

"I have no choice," he said severely.

"You will be returning in the evening then?" Sarah asked.

"It will be impossible for me to look after the required amount of business and get back before the following day," he said.

Abigail spoke up again. "I fear our being left alone."

John frowned. "The servants will all be here. And you have each other for company. You should do very well."

No more was said on the subject, for it was evident he had made up his mind and was in no mood to change it. After dinner they all went their separate ways again, and Sarah was struck by the tense mood that had come over the house.

She said good night to Richard, then went to her own room. She had not been there more than a half hour when there was a soft knock on her door. Rising, she closed the book she'd been reading, and stood with an uneasy expression on her pretty face. The knock was repeated.

"Yes," she said, without moving to open the door. "Who is it?"

"John. May I speak with you a moment?"

She was not pleased by his coming, but did not see how she could directly refuse to open the door to him. She went across, slid back the bolt, and let him in.

He took a step into the room, his handsome face limned in the soft glow from the single lamp on the dresser. "I'm glad to see you bolt your door," he said. "That is wise with vandals about."

Apparently he was determined to keep up the fiction that vandals had entered the house and damaged the portrait. She said, "Isn't it risky to go to Edinburgh and leave Abigail and me in the house with only the child and the servants?"

"I haven't any choice really," John said with an unhappy sigh. "I know you were fond of Rodney, so I hesitate to say anything about him. But he was reckless where money was concerned, and he has two or three gambling debts in Edinburgh that I wish to investigate. There is no other way of doing so aside from going there."

"I see," she said studying him. He seemed to be telling the truth.

"I'll certainly not stay longer than overnight," he said. "In the meantime, take care and I'm sure you'll be all right."

"The house doesn't seem the same without Rodney."

"I miss him more than you can imagine," he said.

"No word from the doctor yet?"

"I spoke to him briefly in the cemetery yesterday," John said. "But he offered me no particulars. MacGregor delights in being secretive."

"Yet I would suppose him to be a very intelligent man."

"He's intelligent enough," John said, with an expression of disdain. "But he does not have a pleasant disposition." He paused. "I must pack for my trip."

"So we may expect you to leave in the morning?"

"I'll be going early," John said. And then taking her in his arms. "And please don't worry your pretty head. Everything will work out all right."

She looked into his eyes. "It is hard to believe that now."

"But it's true," he said. "Just bear with me a little longer. Have faith!" And saying this, he kissed her.

She wanted to break away from him and escape his kiss, but that would let him know that she no longer trusted him or hoped they would enjoy a romance. She wasn't yet ready to reveal that she suspected a sinister collaboration between him and Abigail. It paid to be wary, for she was dealing with someone who had murdered more than once and would not hesitate to do so again. So she submitted to his caresses with a feeling of distress, the same caresses that had once brought her bliss.

When he let her go he stared at her and said, "There seems to be a change in you. I've never found you so cold in my arms."

She looked down. "I suppose it's because I'm still feeling sadness at Rodney's death."

"The circumstances were shocking," John agreed. "His coming to your door and collapsing just outside. What did you tell me his last words were?"

She thought she saw an expression of uneasiness in the handsome face as he carefully put the question. She said, "He seemed to be trying to direct my attention to something. He said, 'The drink,' and then wasn't able to finish."

John shook his head sadly. "You see? He knew himself it was the drink that killed him. That must have been what he was trying to say. If only he'd cut down on his liquor when I suggested it, but he was always stubborn."

"Yes, I suppose he was," she agreed.

He moved to the door. "I'll not keep you from your sleep any longer. And don't let my absence worry you. I'm certain you'll all be perfectly safe." With this final assurance he went out and closed the door.

Sarah went to bed almost immediately after his leaving, but she was not able to sleep. And when it was nearly midnight she again heard the sound of footsteps over her head, a gasping feminine cry of fear, and more weeping. She stared up into the darkness and pondered the mystery. At last the weeping ended and there was only silence again.

Had Abigail found her way upstairs in spite of the new doors and locks John had installed? Were Abigail and John continuing their quarreling? And what were their quarrels about?

Sarah was beginning to wonder if Abigail weren't an unwilling accomplice. It was possible that John had tricked or threatened her into doing his bidding. Perhaps she had been willing to go along with helping bring about Penelope's death in the belief the handsome master of Dankhurst would marry her. And when he had made no move to do this, and then had brought Sarah to the house, the attractive girl might have become jealous and the quarreling began. And it could be that Abigail was shattered by the plot against Rodney. She might have balked at conspiring against the likable young man, who also offered a romantic possibility for her.

Maybe some shrewd questioning might make Abigail reveal some of these things. That could be the beginning of a plan to bring John Stone's evil out into the open. And thinking thus, Sarah determined to put some blunt queries to the girl as soon as John was safely on his way to Edinburgh. Abigail would be on the defensive once she was left alone. With these thoughts Sarah fell into a deep sleep.

But it did not work out as she had hoped. When she went down to breakfast the next morning, ready to question Abigail, there was no sign of her. Mrs. Fergus told her why. "Miss Abigail is in her room with a sick headache."

"Is she really ill?" Sarah asked.

"She ate a good enough breakfast," Mrs. Fergus said, removing Sarah's porridge plate and replacing it with a dish of toast and sausage. "It's my belief she's more lazy than anything else."

Sarah knew this was as much as she could expect from the usually taciturn Mrs. Fergus.

As the day was fine, she and Richard went to the rose garden for the morning lessons. She gave him a series of problems in arithmetic, and while he worked on them she read from one of Mr. Dickens' novels. She was deep in a most exciting passage when she heard the sound of a carriage at the front of the house. Closing the book, she rose to walk to a spot where she could see who it was.

A moment later the severe Dr. Mac-Gregor came striding purposefully around the corner of the house. On seeing her, he headed for the rose garden. Richard had already abandoned his arithmetic lessons, happy at the distraction, and was running to greet the doctor.

Dr. MacGregor offered the boy a patronizing smile. "Well," he said, "it seems we are much improved."

"I feel a lot better," Richard assured him, walking shyly at his side as they came over to Sarah.

The doctor removed his hat and bowed to her, the bearded face impassive. "Well, Miss Bennett, it seems I could have skipped this call without doing any harm. The boy is recovering nicely."

"He is, Doctor," she assured him.

"Since I'm here, I had better have a talk with Mr. Stone."

"I'm sorry," Sarah said. "Mr. Stone had to go to Edinburgh. He won't be returning until tomorrow."

"Gone to Edinburgh?" The doctor sounded astonished.

"Yes. He took the early morning train."

"He didn't mention it to me yesterday," Dr. MacGregor said. "I expect it was a sudden decision."

"I believe so," she said. Then turning to the boy, she said, "Richard, why don't you go to the kitchen and have Mrs. Fergus get you a shortbread and a glass of milk." Richard needed no second bidding and sped off in the direction of the kitchen at once. Sarah now turned to the doctor. "I believe you have come here with serious news, Doctor. And I also would like to tell you a few things."

The bearded man showed no expression, but his sharp eyes were studying her. "Really! Is that why you got rid of the boy just now?"

"Yes."

"Pray be seated, Miss Bennett. You interest me greatly." He waved her to the wooden bench. She seated herself again and stared up at him with a grave face.

"Rodney Stone died from the effects of poisoned liquor, didn't he?"

Dr. MacGregor's eyebrows raised. "Is that your opinion, young lady?"

"Yes, it is. I'm sure he didn't suffer a natural death, because of the many things that have been happening in this house."

"Indeed?"

"I don't know what it means. But I'm sure there have been a series of poisonings — first, John Stone's wife, Penelope;

256

then attempts on their son; and the other day, Rodney."

The bearded face showed wry interest. "Your mind runs to poisonings, doesn't it Miss Bennett? But then I suppose that is only natural, considering your unfortunate experience."

"I was brought here for some purpose," she said tensely.

"But of course: to look after young Richard."

"Some purpose beyond that!"

"Well, I really can't offer an opinion on that," Dr. MacGregor said easily. "But I can tell you your suspicions concerning Rodney's death are well-founded."

"I knew it!"

"Rodney Stone did die of poisoned liquor," the doctor said evenly, "although how you knew it I will not venture to guess."

"It had to be," she said. "He was stricken so suddenly."

The doctor was watching her with an odd expression. "I came to inform Mr. Stone of the fact, and had intended to let him know I have sent the results of my autopsy, along with the remainder of the poisoned liquor, to the proper authorities. They will no doubt be taking steps at once."

"Poor Rodney!" she murmured.

Dr. MacGregor nodded. "Poor Rodney, indeed! Under ordinary circumstances I would not have revealed this to you. But since you already seem to be in possession of the facts, I can't see that it will do any harm."

She leaned forward anxiously. "There are other things you should know, Doctor. For the safety of the boy."

"Such as?"

"He has told me his mother comes to him in the night. And I don't think he is making up a story; every detail is correct. A few times she brought him a drink, and it was after these visits that he became ill."

"What an unusual story," Dr. Mac-Gregor said.

"I have warned him to refuse any food or drink if she comes again," Sarah went on.

Dr. MacGregor listened with narrowed eyes. "Fantastic!" he said. "Utterly fantastic!"

"And there are other things, Doctor. I must hurry to tell you before Richard gets back! Strange weeping in the attic above me at night; talk of the spirit of Priscilla Kirk returning to avenge herself on the house; a stone sarcophagus, in an attic room, from which I saw an emaciated hand emerge. And I was attacked by a phantom at least three times!"

Dr. MacGregor gazed down at her in open consternation. "Are you sure you are not allowing yourself to be confused?"

"I'm telling you what has been happening," she said, rising. "You must believe me."

"You will admit you are offering me some bizarre information, Miss Bennett."

She leaned close to him. "I think John Stone and Abigail Durmot are in it together. And unless the authorities act at once it won't stop with Rodney's death. I know it."

Dr. MacGregor frowned at her; suddenly he raised his hand in warning. She turned and saw Mrs. Fergus, tight-mouthed and sour as usual, walking primly toward them.

Sarah went to meet her. "Did you give Richard his treat? I told him you would."

"Yes," the old woman said. "That is not why I am here. Master Richard said the doctor had come and I wanted to let you know that Miss Abigail has been taken worse!"

Dr. MacGregor stepped forward quickly. "What is this about Abigail Durmot?"

"I'd forgotten," Sarah faltered. "She had a headache this morning. But I didn't think she was really very ill."

"She is now," Mrs. Fergus said crisply. "And she's asking for the doctor."

Dr. MacGregor gave Sarah a sharp glance. "Maybe it's fortunate I arrived when I did, after all," he said. And he followed Mrs. Fergus inside to see to Abigail.

Sarah assigned some new problems to Richard, and then hurried into the house to await word on Abigail's condition. She was standing in the central hallway when Dr. MacGregor came downstairs.

"How is she?" she asked.

"Dangerously ill," the doctor said, a gleam of anger in his eyes. "I doubt if she'll recover."

Fear trickled across Sarah's lovely face. "What is wrong?" she asked in a bare whisper.

The doctor came close to her and said sternly, "Arsenic, Miss Bennett! That's what is wrong! The same poison again! I may as well tell you I believe you are a little mad, young woman! And I think you are responsible for the poisonings that have been going on in this house!"

12

Sarah recoiled in shock. "No!" she exclaimed, lifting a hand to her mouth in an agonized gesture.

"You deny it then, Miss Bennett?" The bearded doctor's tone was harsh, and their voices echoed in the hallway.

"Whatever has gone on, I've had nothing to do with it!" she pleaded.

His smile was derisive. "No, Miss Bennett, you have been too busy with phantom figures emerging from stone coffins, wraiths paying visits to young children, Priscilla Kirk's spirit returning to hack a portrait to bits!"

"I told you those things to try and make you understand!"

"I understand only too well," Dr. MacGregor snapped. "I say you are mad, Miss Bennett. And I warn you that as soon as John Stone returns I intend to tell him so. You may be sure the authorities will be here to ask you some interesting questions."

"It is you who must be mad if you think I'm the guilty one," she retorted with spirit. "Ask your questions of John Stone! Ask him what caused his wife's death!"

"I intend to," Dr. MacGregor assured her, his bearded face livid. "But that has nothing to do with these recent events. You can pray that Abigail Durmot recovers and that you are able to offer some suitable explanation in the case of Rodney Stone's death."

"Rodney tried to tell me about the poison, but he died before he was able to," she said, sobbing.

"A likely story," the doctor said. "It's no good, young woman! I had you marked down as a dangerous madwoman from the time of your trial in Edinburgh. It was a miscarriage of justice that you were allowed to go free. And now we have to pay the penalty for your madness."

He railed at her for several minutes as she covered her face with her hands, sobbing her innocence. When she realized he had finally returned upstairs to his patient she managed to get control of herself and go out to Richard in the rose garden. Trying to hide her misery, she told him that lessons were finished for the day and gave him permission to go to the stables and see the horses and spend some time with the friendly groom.

Then she sought the refuge of her own room. She threw herself on her bed and sobbed some more. And now she could see the pattern that had eluded her taking shape. John Stone had brought her to Dankhurst because he intended to continue his career as a poisoner. He had neatly gotten rid of Penelope that way using the senile Dr. Gideon to cover up his crime.

But he couldn't depend on that same device when he killed his son and Rodney. Madman that he must be, he had enough cunning to see that he must have a scapegoat in the house. So he had come to her trial with the idea of pretending to befriend her if she should be freed. The old judge had unwittingly played into his hands and turned her over to him. Once in the house he had proceeded with his insane plans, intending that Sarah should be blamed for the new poisonings. Oh, it was all so clear to her now.

That was why he had suddenly given way to her pleas to call in Dr. MacGregor, for he had cast him to play a part in the drama he was arranging. Dr. MacGregor was the one who would suspect her and turn her over to the police. Suspicion would then be neatly diverted from him, and she would face another trial in which she would surely be declared guilty.

She had been subjected to all those strange events so she would tell of her experiences and thus cast doubt on her sanity. She did not fully know the meaning of Abigail's illness. She would have expected John to spare his wife's attractive cousin, as his infatuation for her had likely been the start of all this. Then again, perhaps the quarrels in the attic had been real, and John was using this means of ridding himself of the girl and letting Sarah take the blame for her, as well. Or it could be an even more subtle scheme. Perhaps Abigail had taken just enough of the poison to make herself ill without endangering her life. This way, guilt would fall on Sarah, but Abigail would make a recovery.

The more Sarah thought about it, the more convinced she was that she had blundered into a web of evil from which it was impossible to extricate herself. She had no friends left to turn to, so she was completely at the mercy of her accusers. And she could count on John Stone to pretend shock and sympathy while making her case look as bad as possible.

This was the hardest of all to accept. She had looked on the handsome blond John as a knight in shining armor. She had been ready to fall in love with him, willing to entrust her future to him. And all the time he had been viciously plotting against her!

She stayed in her room sitting by the window. At dinner time Mrs. Fergus came up and knocked on her door to inquire if she would be coming down for the evening meal. When she replied in the negative, Mrs. Fergus promised she would bring her up some tea and toast.

Which she did. And when she left the tray, she told Sarah, "The doctor is going to stay all night. He says he may be able to pull Miss Abigail through."

"Thank you, Mrs. Fergus," she said.

The old woman gave her a grim nod. "I warned you," she said. "I told you at the first you shouldn't stay here."

"So you did," Sarah recalled. "Why?"

The nut-brown face was set in hard lines. "I had good reasons," she said, and started to leave.

Sarah followed her to the door. "What were your reasons?"

The old woman shook her head. "It makes no difference now. It's too late." And she went on out.

Sarah had little sleep that night. And close to midnight it began to rain and the rain continued right on through till morning. Several times she was certain she heard movements in the attic above her, but she knew she must be wrong. With John Stone in Edinburgh, who would have a key to go up there?

When morning finally arrived it was still drizzling rain, and Sarah's mood was as miserable as the weather. Mrs. Fergus brought her up her tea and told her Dr. MacGregor wished to see her downstairs.

She dressed slowly and looked at the pale drawn face and red swollen eyes in the mirror. She was showing her ordeal only too plainly. With reluctance, she went down to face the bearded doctor.

He was waiting for her in the living room, standing under the portrait of the glum old Stephen Dank. He gave her a nod as she came across the living room to him.

"I have some interesting news for you," he said.

"Please be brief," she told him.

He smiled coldly. "Anything to oblige a lady. You will be pleased to know Abigail Durmot is going to recover."

"That doesn't surprise me."

"No? Because you knew you hadn't

266

made the dose of arsenic strong enough?"

"Because I didn't think she intended to risk her life," Sarah said with a wise look. "She took only enough of the poison to make her a little ill and get your sympathy. More of their scheme to point the finger of guilt at me."

"Where I think it belongs! Your story of Abigail Durmot taking the poison herself is as twisted as the rest of your fables."

"I've told you the truth," she insisted hotly.

"And I don't believe you," the doctor said. "I'm remaining until John Stone gets here, and placing all the facts before him."

"Then you are remaining to meet the murderer," she said with angry despair.

"I shall tell him of your accusations," Dr. MacGregor assured her. "And I doubt if it will be beneficial to you. In the meantime, I shall expect you to keep yourself ready to join Mr. Stone and myself when he arrives, at which time I will offer him my version of what has been going on here."

She turned and went up the stairs without replying. It was working out exactly as she'd expected. A cunning Abigail had taken just enough poison to make her ill and draw Dr. MacGregor's attention — and sympathy. Once he had the idea of

267

Sarah being the guilty one in his head, John and Abigail's plan was complete. But not quite: the boy still lived.

Feeling a surge of affection for little Richard, she went directly to his room. He was on the floor playing with a set of blocks, with which he had made a fort, and his toy soldiers. Seeing her enter, he got up.

"Are they mad at you, Sarah?" he asked worriedly.

She patted his head. "It doesn't matter."

"It does too!" he said, determinedly. "I won't let them be mean to you. And when my father gets back he'll make that doctor stop calling you names."

Sarah forced a smile. "It isn't important. I think we'll do our lessons right in your room today. It's still drizzling outside."

Richard nodded, looking unhappy. "Mrs. Fergus says they should burn you for a witch. And I told her she looked more like one than you did."

She was sorting out his books on the dresser and she spoke to him over her shoulder. "You shouldn't be saucy to your elders, including Mrs. Fergus."

"She's not right in the head!" Richard said, his small face solemn. "My father said so."

"Oh, he did, did he?" she turned with the arithmetic book open. "I think we'd better get our mind on other things."

She was still in Richard's room when John returned. She heard the carriage and watched from the upstairs window as he alighted from it, a striking figure in his gray coat and top hat. It was still drizzling rain and her mood was in keeping with the day. Turning to the boy, she quickly finished with his lesson, certain that she would be summoned downstairs in a few minutes.

Her expectation proved correct. A nervous little maid tapped at the door and informed her, "The master would like to see you in the study."

Richard looked up at her worriedly. "Can I go with you and tell my father about the doctor being mean to you?"

She smiled sadly and touched his blond head. "Because this is something I can do better by myself. You keep reading awhile."

She left the boy with his books, feeling much less confident than she had pretended. As she reached the foot of the stairs she was trembling, and she tried to steel herself for the confrontation with the doctor and John Stone.

The study door was open and a troubled John came quickly to show her in. He said,

"It seems I was wrong in leaving, after all. This is distressing news about Abigail."

She made no reply, but went on into the room; he closed the door behind her to insure privacy. The doctor was standing by the fireplace, a sour expression on his bearded face.

John motioned her to a chair. "Pray, do sit down, Sarah, until we hear the doctor out." John took a stand beside her chair.

Dr. MacGregor cleared his throat, and with his hands clasped behind his back, said, "I thought I made myself clear before you brought Miss Bennett down. It is my belief she poisoned your brother and attempted to take Miss Durmot's life in the same fashion."

Crimson spots showed on John's face. "That is a preposterous statement, Mac-Gregor," he said with some anger. "You must be daft to accuse Sarah in this manner."

Somewhat surprised at his defense of her, Sarah glanced up at his troubled features. Then she decided that this was all part of the game. He was going to feign shock and horror before he finally agreed with the doctor as to her guilt. She looked down at the carpet in dull misery.

Dr. MacGregor sounded coldly menacing. "I warn you, it will be best if you don't take too strong a stand in this, Mr. Stone. You're not entirely in the clear yourself. There is the matter of your wife's mysterious death. I don't have to tell you there is much gossip in the village as to what caused her passing."

"No one can prove that Penelope died of anything but natural causes," John said, growing more incensed. "I have Dr. Gideon's certificate to back me in this. I will not be cowed by your repeating malicious village talk."

"Dr. Gideon is senile, sir," MacGregor said. "And it is still possible for the body of your wife to be exhumed and perhaps found to contain the same arsenic that has done the rest of the damage here."

John hesitated, obviously taken aback; in a low voice he asked, "What are you trying to tell me?"

"That you would be wise not to attempt to bluster this out," Dr. MacGregor informed him. "I believe this young woman to be mentally unsound. I think she has a mania for poisoning that makes her a menace. I shall report these beliefs to the authorities, and you, sir, would be wise not to interfere."

"I see," John Stone said quietly. "You are

actually planning to put this poor girl through more torment on a mere guess."

"The poisoned liquor and your half brother's death from it is a fact," the doctor said. "Abigail Durmot's suffering from the same arsenic poisoning is a fact; and your son's being a victim of an identical poison is yet another fact."

"But how can you connect Sarah with all this?" John Stone wanted to know.

"Because I believe she was guilty of murder in the Gordon case," Dr. MacGregor told him. "I cannot understand your perversity in bringing her here as a governess to your son and giving her an opportunity to do more deviltry, unless —" he stopped short.

John Stone stared at him. "Unless what?"

The doctor shrugged. "Unless it was a case of like seeking like," he said with meaning. "Why your deep interest in this young woman?"

"Because, unlike you, I do not think she was guilty," John said with a show of defiance that startled Sarah. "And because I wished to help her."

"Commendable," Dr. MacGregor said, "but hardly convincing."

John turned to Sarah. "What do you say to all this?"

She raised her head, with proud courage, and said, "I have already told Dr. Mac-Gregor he is wrong."

"And a good deal more," the doctor snapped. "I will not go into that now. I do not choose to enter into a round of recriminations. But I should like to search Miss Bennett's room."

"Why?" John demanded.

"You ask for evidence to link her with these crimes. I believe we may find some there."

John looked astonished, and asked her, "Do you object, Sarah?"

She still had the feeling this was a charade in which she played her role whether she wanted to or not. She mistrusted John and did not know what turn the drama would take next. But realizing that it was pointless to protest, she said, "Very well! He may search my room if he likes."

She and John took no active part in the careful going over of her possessions. They stood by the door as Dr. MacGregor searched every nook and cranny thoroughly. When he had completed his fruitless investigation of her room he turned his attention to the closet. Sarah watched with horrified fascination as he delved into every corner of it. Suddenly he turned around to face her, a triumphant smile on his face, and a round flat can in his hand.

"What have we here, Miss Bennett?" he asked. Opening the can, he held out the sooty-looking contents for both her and John to see. "Arsenic, my dear young lady. Arsenic, mixed with a touch of soot to color it — the type obtainable at any apothecary's." He glanced at John, "Are you satisfied now, Mr. Stone?"

John looked shocked. Sarah judged it a neat bit of playacting. This would be the moment he denounced her. But instead he said, "What do you say, Sarah?"

"I don't know anything about it," she said. "I've never seen it before."

Dr. MacGregor laughed harshly. "You can't really expect us to believe that?"

"I do," John said with surprising vehemence, making Sarah wonder what new trick he might have in mind. "I think Sarah is telling the truth."

"I see," Dr. MacGregor nodded, placing the tin in the pocket of his tweed jacket. "In any case, it is not for me to argue with you about this. I will notify the authorities, and you can be sure the police will be out here in the morning. You had better be prepared!" And with this warning he went out of the room.

John followed him. "Are you leaving now?"

The doctor paused and turned. "There is no need for me to remain any longer. Miss Durmot is recovering nicely, and I have all the evidence I require to substantiate my accusations." With a sour smile, he nodded and went on down the corridor.

John turned to her in bewilderment and placed a comforting arm around her. "I will correct this injustice," he promised.

His lips gently touched her hair in a gesture of reassurance. But to her it was a mockery; she still believed that he was deliberately using her to take the blame for his deeds. Complaining of a headache, she insisted on remaining in her room alone. Once more she did not go down to dinner, and Mrs. Fergus again brought her a well-filled tray of food.

When that worthy came back for the tray she gave Sarah a grim look and informed her, "Master took his dinner in Miss Abigail's room."

"I'm not surprised," Sarah said.

Fog followed the drizzle of rain, and darkness came early. She tried to read the novel by Dickens, but her own plight was now so distressing that she was unable to concentrate. Yet she felt so little like sleeping that she sat until it was long past her usual bedtime, with the open book on her lap. The lamp on the dresser cast a dim light over the room, and she wondered if she would be there another night or in some bare cell in the Rawlwyn jail.

She was still sitting in the chair when she heard John's footsteps coming along the hall. She listened, thinking he might pause by her door, but he didn't. She heard the padlock rattle as he unlocked it and slipped it from its place, and then his measured tread as he went upstairs.

So he was going to spend some midnight hours at his black sorcery! She was beginning to feel that all the evil in the old mansion was centered up there in that attic. The musty smell of the room with the sarcophagus came vividly back to her, as did the shuddering memory of that black creature she had seen crawling swiftly across a crate to vanish in the shadows. And the weird apparition that had attacked her!

These morbid thoughts were passing through her mind as she waited to hear sounds from above. And at last they came — the shuffling of feet, the rumble of John's deep voice, and the lighter tones of a woman. Was Abigail well enough to be up there? It seemed unlikely. But it must be Abigail, for who else —

Suddenly she heard a heavy thud followed by a woman's piercing scream! Sarah jumped up from her chair her lovely face showing terror. Now there was silence. She stood there with the feeling she had been a party to some dark deed, that some horror had been perpetrated above that had a bearing on her.

And then the footsteps came along the hall. She was certain it was John again. Cautiously she moved to place her ear against the door. The soft knock on the panel where she rested her ear almost made her step back in fright.

"Is that you, John?" she asked.

The answer came in a hoarse whisper, "Yes."

What had happened above? Why was he whispering in this strange manner? Had some dreadful thing happened to Abigail? Her mind raced with one thought following swiftly on another.

"What is wrong?" she asked, hesitating, her hand resting on the bolt.

"Please!" It was an urgent whisper this time.

John must have been injured, perhaps stabbed by a maddened Abigail. And all her hatred vanished, along with her fear, in a rush of concern for the man she had loved. With trembling fingers she slid back the bolt and opened the door to help him.

But it wasn't John who advanced into the room!

This was sheer horror that moved toward her! A phantom figure of stench, tattered clothes, and a heavy dark veil over its head! It was the figure of a woman, and in her raised, clawlike hand gleamed a dagger.

Sarah screamed in terror and backed up. The creature pursued her with a maniacal laugh and raised the dagger high to plunge it into her. She grappled with the foul-smelling phantom, fighting to hold back the dagger; and in the struggle the veil slipped off her attacker's head.

With a cry of dismay the creature broke away, and Sarah had a frightening look at her ravaged face. For a moment she almost called out Priscilla Kirk's name, so much did the scarred, mutilated features resemble those of the plaster statue on the lawn. But although the horror had a familiar look, it was not Priscilla Kirk she resembled.

With sudden recognition, Sarah whispered, "Justine!"

Justine the beautiful! Justine of the portrait's arrogant smile! Now a scarred grotesque, without a nose, with cheeks misshapen and withered, with her head bald except for a few stray wisps of hair, with her mouth crumpled and shrunken!

Sarah heard a maniacal cackle from the creature who had once been John's lovely half sister and who now advanced on her with the dagger ready to thrust again. As Sarah backed the short remaining distance to the window she saw John over the apparition's shoulder. His head was bloodied, as if from a severe blow, and his face was deathly white.

He came into the room quickly, shouting, "Justine!"

The phantom wheeled and uttered a hoarse cry of dismay. He came close to her, and after a brief struggle wrenched the dagger from her hand. Justine gave another despairing cry, then turned and ran from the room. John followed her, only to return a moment later.

Going over to a trembling Sarah, he said, "She's gone downstairs. She'll run off into the darkness. She can't bear to have anyone see her. I'll go find her as soon as I know you're all right."

She stared up at him, dazed with fright and the ugly revelation. "Justine!" she whispered. "How long has she been up there?"

"Too long," he said solemnly. "She wasn't killed in that fire in France. Only scarred and maddened. I brought her back here to care for her, but it was a mistake. She plotted against Penelope and caused her death. I didn't realize until she taunted me with it afterward."

Sarah shook her head. "Why didn't you send her away then?"

"Put her in a madhouse?" he said sadly. "I hoped to avoid it. She had committed this crime out of her insane love for me. She promised to remain upstairs and never do such a thing again. But she had no intention of keeping the promise. I should have known that."

"And it was she who visited Richard?"

"Yes."

"And poisoned Rodney, and tried to do the same to Abigail?"

"All true," John said grimly. "And it was she who attacked you and planted the poison in your room. She was afraid you might escape being accused for her crimes, knowing that I would protect her no longer. So tonight she waited to strike me down when I visited her, and then came here to finish you."

"I should have guessed when you had the new doors installed," Sarah said.

"A puny measure to combat such a threat as Justine presented," was John's reply. "Now I must go and bring her back."

Sarah followed him to the door. "What will you do this time?"

"I have no choice. I'll do what I should have done before. Turn her over to the police with a full account of how I've tried to protect her. I can no longer save her from a madhouse."

But it was not to work out that way. Though he and two of the servants searched the grounds for hours, they did not find Justine. The following morning a farmer near the river found her body. She had evidently fled to the river to drown herself, as the legendary Priscilla Kirk had done years before. But she had not managed it. Instead, she'd toppled down a steep hill of rocks in her frantic flight, and crushed her head in the fall.

With the death of Justine and the clearing of the mystery Dankhurst no longer remained a house of brooding evil. Richard grew stronger and healthier each day, and at Sarah's request John promised to have the more macabre of his Egyptian items sent to a museum. It was an easy decision for him, for he now was much more interested in the present and his future with her than he was in the past.

The attractive Abigail, whom Sarah had unjustly suspected of conspiring in murder and working against her, was quick to sense the happy new atmosphere in the towering gray mansion.

She came to Sarah in the garden one afternoon, and with a smile, said, "I'm leaving in a few days. My aunt wishes me to join her in London."

"We shall miss you."

"Not that much," Abigail said with a knowing expression. "I wish you and John every happiness. You are so surely the right person for him."

And so it came that one day in September Sarah and John journeyed to Edinburgh with Abigail to see her safely on the train to London. It was a crisp bright day with a blue sky overhead, and Sarah thought she had never truly seen Edinburgh before.

When the train pulled out of the busy station they returned to their carriage, and John instructed the driver to take them to Edinburgh Castle. The wind blew at the trimmings of her bonnet as she sat close to him.

And then they were standing together on

the ramparts of the castle, staring down at the lovely old city. In the castle courtyard there were colorful kilted Highland militia, and the wail of bagpipes reached their ears. His hand held hers as they stared down at the sober majesty of the landscape below. There was the Royal Mile, Holyrood Palace, Parliament Square, and the gardens and smart shops of Princes Street.

John smiled down at her. "Will you ever be able to think of this old city kindly after all the trouble you've known here?"

It was one of the few smiles he'd offered her, and she could do no less than return it and say, "You forget that it brought me happiness and you!"

And in a gesture quite out of keeping with any tradition of dour Scotsmen, he boldly took her in his arms then and there, and planted a kiss on her lovely lips for all Auld Reekie to see.

We hope you have enjoyed this Large Print book. Other Thorndike, Wheeler or Chivers Press Large Print books are available at your library or directly from the publishers.

For more information about current and upcoming titles, please call or write, without obligation, to:

Publisher
Thorndike Press
295 Kennedy Memorial Drive
Waterville, ME   04901
Tel. (800) 223-1244

Or visit our Web site at:
www.gale.com/thorndike
www.gale.com/wheeler

OR

Chivers Large Print
published by BBC Audiobooks Ltd
St James House, The Square
Lower Bristol Road
Bath BA2 3SB
England
Tel. +44(0) 800 136919
email: bbcaudiobooks@bbc.co.uk
www.bbcaudiobooks.co.uk

All our Large Print titles are designed for easy reading, and all our books are made to last.